NO CENTURY FOR APOLOGIES

Jack Remick

ONE

Castle lay on the bed listening to TV. Eyes closed, he translated the dialogue into Aymara. He knew there was no word in Aymara for pantyhose, while underarm deodorant made no sense in any language. He muted the TV.

When the knock came Castle didn't move. A big man might have yanked open the door, but impulsiveness was a luxury only for big men. There are no reckless mice, no slow shrews. Being small had its disadvantages. You were either fast or you were dead.

"Castle."

Not good. They said they'd call. No one said anything about coming to get him. Small animals will fake death. Castle was good at it. Don't move, they can't see you. Don't breathe, they can't hear your breath. Castle, like any small creature when trapped by the big man, froze.

"Castle."

On the television, a young woman dressed like a Colombian peasant delivered a singing coffee commercial.

"Castle, I know you're in there."

They knew his name. Biggs. Castle moved to the door. He released the chain and stood back.

A short man strode in. Eye to eye with Castle. He puffed his chest out. A man with an air of confidence out of synch with his voice.

"Biggs said they'd call," Castle said.

"I'm here."

Castle survived because he heard the whisper beneath the words. Words masked truth, but the feelings under them never lied. It was this deep listening that accounted for Castle's success at what he did.

Looking at Shorty was like looking at a naked sword. Shorty said,

"Get your shit together."

"Who sent you?"

"Clock's running."

Castle grabbed the small bag from the bed.

"That's it?"

—Where are we going? — Castle said in Quechua.

"Whaz that?"

"Where to?" Castle said. Shorty didn't speak Quechua.

******

A limousine was parked in front of the hotel. Castle withdrew into his chameleon skin, his gray side up. He made a habit of becoming what the unspoken signs demanded, and right then they demanded invisibility.

Shorty smoked as they pushed through traffic. Castle noted that he wasn't smoking American cigarettes. Piel Rojas. The sweet smell of the tobacco filled the car.

The little man did not speak until they stopped at the Centrex building.

******

Randall stood at the filing cabinet, a white silk scarf draped around her neck. Diamond specks sparkled in her ear lobes. Even at midnight, she looked as crisp as she had the morning before when, on two hours' sleep, she brought him from the hotel to the interview with Biggs.

"They're waiting," she said.

Cold and efficient as if she didn't recognize him. She nodded at the door.

Two men in dark suits framed the doorway. One of them was tall, the other taller. Business was written all over them the way death etches time on an undertaker's face. The tall one's suit said he was important. His shoes said he was very important. His hands said he was more important than the taller one.

"You'll be with Everett," taller one said. "This way."

*****

The tall man, when Shorty and Castle and the taller man were in the hallway, sat down in the chair. He said,

"What do you think, Randall?"

"He has experience," she said. "He speaks seven languages. Of all the candidates, he's the most qualified."

"Kinda short, isn't he?"

"Tall enough," Randall said.

"Does he have character?"

"He has the survival instincts of a wild pig and the stamina of a mustang."

The tall man smiled. He said,

"A woman sleeps with a man once and she knows everything about him. How does that work?"

"Stickiness," Randall said.

"Stickiness?"

"Will he stick around when you're pregnant."

"Will he?"

Randall opened a cabinet and took down two snifters which she filled with brandy. She said,

"He's fierce." She glanced at the door.

TWO

Castle followed Shorty and the taller man down the corridor. The man said,

"You'll be with Everett."

"You're not Everett," Castle said.

"I'm not Everett."

"Who is Everett?"

"Shut up," Shorty said.

"When do I start?" Castle said

"You've started," Shorty said. "Gimme your passport."

He opened a door with the word DOCUMENTS in gold lettering.

A lone man sat at a desk, a lamp placed so Castle couldn't see his face. His hand came out of the shadow. He stamped Castle's passport then handed it back to Shorty who handed it to Castle. Shorty herded Castle back into the corridor.

Castle glanced at the passport. The visa was stamped Republica de Ayahuantu. Ayahuantu the second smallest, the second poorest of the mid-continent small, poor countries. A population just over half a million. Castle spoke three of the four languages there. The question was, what did Centrex have going in Ayahuantu?

The taller man vanished leaving Castle's suitcase with Shorty. Castle said,

"My suitcase?"

Shorty punched the street level elevator button

******

7

In the limousine, Castle said,

"Where to now?"

Shorty looked straight ahead and lit a Piel Roja. Castle studied his face in the moving light of the nighttime city.

Shorty was under 40. In good shape. His face rugged, worn out. Muscular. Square hands with small tufts of reddish hair on the backs of the fingers. He wore a herringbone tweed jacket, black slacks, white shirt, red and yellow tie in a half-Windsor. He reeked of information. Castle said,

"You're company security?"

"Look, bud, you make my life complicated. I don't like you, I don't want you to like me. My job is to get you where you're supposed to be."

THREE

The jet touched down on a small strip.

The pilot shut down the engines. Everett peered out the porthole.

After a few minutes, the big man opened the hatch and stood in the doorway.

Rows of small planes lined the parking area.

The sharp twitter of night birds knifed through the air.

"Where are we?" Castle said.

"Miami," Everett replied.

He lowered the jetway. In a rasped whisper as if he was afraid of being overheard, he said,

"Truck on over to the shack. Get us a taxi. Take this with you."

He thrust the briefcase at Castle.

As Castle approached the shack, he scanned the area. The shack looked empty. The windsock still.

Secrecy. It was what he did well. Doing what was asked of him. He had been used this way before. Everett wanted anonymity. He wanted secrecy. What the secret was made no difference. Castle was, at this moment an extension of the big man. Until they had accomplished what Everett had set out to do, that was all he would be.

Behind him, the airplane squatted, a blood-sucking insect on an expanse of black skin.

******

Because he was a small man, Castle needed to appear harmless to people he met for the first time. He imagined that he had chameleon genes in his past. He squirmed his way into any stranger's confidence with a few words or perhaps it was the way he held his body—at once non-threatening yet solid, exact and soft, the demeanor of a man used to working with vicious animals who smell fear, sense timidity, despise indecision.

In this way, Castle softened the edges of the cabbie's curiosity when he got in the front seat beside him.

A veteran of the night and living at the edge of the underground, the cabbie talked, forgetting about the big man in the back seat.

Castle had traded the brashness of the large for the finesse of the petit and he used words the way a cat in the darkness hunts, its whiskers tracking movement, his nose the smells of a moving universe. To Castle, vision was cloudy and meant little while words were more than sounds to him. Words had a voluptuous reality to him—like ripe melon or clusters of grapes. He often felt words moving in his brain before they became sound. They were tangible beings at work in him as they melted in the chemical stew of neurons and axons and neurotransmitters and synapses. He never knew with certainty the moment when he merged with the consciousness of the man beside him, but at a certain time, they became as alike as brothers—speaking the same language, feeling the same vibrations, tasting the same bite of time and in that time becoming a duplicate living in the shadow of his brother's private existence.

Feeling the young man's strength, Castle became pliant. To deal with a hard man, Castle became soft. He had the ability to concentrate on the short term, to attend to the tale being told as though it were the most important event in human history. When he was working, Castle never dismissed anyone as insignificant because he never knew who might become a shield and at the moment, no one was more important than the cabbie because he was information. He was insight. He was the future unfolding mile by mile. Later, he would be less valuable as he slid into a past as Castle turned into action. Castle fed on the future like a saprophyte feeding on the sap of a vigorous tree. In becoming like the other, only rarely did one destroy one's self.

A hand on his shoulder brought Castle back to the big man behind him. A note. On the paper was the name of a hotel.

—You know it? —Castle asked the cabbie.

—Sure, it's in Little Havana. But you don't want to stay there. —

—Why not? —

—It's one of the worst hotels in Miami. What's he into? —

—The old man? —

—Drugs? —

—I think he wants to buy the Panama Canal. —

******

Once a respectable second-class hotel, the Leamington had decayed into a greying stack of worn carpets, chipped marble stairways and baroque chandeliers. Castle knew that the bathroom fixtures would be stained and the faucets would drip.

The clientele were older women whose blond hair showed a dark past. The body no longer fetched the money it once did. Everything sagged closer to perdition and there was no reprieve.

You did not go to the Leamington unless you were looking for someone or something.

Everett hung back while Castle asked for rooms using a name which was not his own. This did not surprise the desk clerk. Castle knew she would not remember them in the daylight but would recall only that one of them was short, the other tall.

******

In the elevator, Everett said,

"We're changing rooms. Give me your key."

He unlocked a room as ripe as a mausoleum. Ancient paper peeled from damp walls. Floral print drapes trapped a light layer of dust in their folds.

Everett dropped his suitcase at the foot of a bed that sagged in the middle. He crossed to the window. He said,

"I'll stay put. You take charge. I won't go down for meals."

"Room service?"

"No."

Everett shed his jacket, loosened his tie. He said,

"Round me up something. I'm going to catch a few winks."

"Anything special?"

"No chilis, no beans. See what you can do. I'll want a taxi at six. In the alley. I'll go down the fire stairs."

Everett handed Castle five fifty-dollar bills. He lay on the bed and closed his eyes. Castle started for the door. Everett said,

"Six o'clock. And leave the briefcase, Castle."

******

Castle knew Miami. He knew people there. Some of the people he knew were women. Ana Magdalena Velasquez was one of those women. He wanted to see her, but Ana Magdalena Velasquez was not an easy women to see because her guardian was a cruel man who made his living trading other people's weaknesses and secrets to men who lived on secrets and weakness, a man who understood the larcenous nature of men, a man who ought never to have married a jewel like Ana nor done business with a man such as Castle.

Her voice was hesitant when he called to ask if she would meet him. She told him Arnolfo was away. She didn't know where he was, she didn't know when he would return but he had hired a man to watch her. No. It would not be difficult to get away.

******

Ana was a small woman. Her eyes sparkled when she entered Castle's room at the Leamington. There was a softness in the way she walked that made Castle think she was moving in slow motion. Ana had the ability to project the innocent urgency of a young girl while moving with the ageless wisdom of a woman experienced in the pain of living. She lingered in the mind like evening flowered perfume. She said,

—You are different, Castle. —

—And you have not changed. —

—Perhaps it is that you have become more of what you were before,— she said. –Where are you going now? —

Castle hesitated but he knew that anything he told her would die with her. Her secrecy was of a kind that hid behind her innocence. Castle said,

—Ayahuantu. —

—Ayahuantu is an ugly place now. —

—Everywhere is ugly now,— Castle said. –Is Arnolfo still selling weapons? —

—This man you are with, does he sell death? —

—He tells me only what I need to know,—Castle said.

—You are a strange one, Castillo. —

—My work means nothing. It can never mean anything. It is only what I do. —

—A man must have purpose. Arnolfo too. He too is death. I hate him. —

—Leave with me. —

—He would have someone kill me. A man like you, perhaps. Would you kill me for sleeping with other men? —

—No. —

—I don't know why I sleep with men. Men are only anguish. It is a terrible thing to be human now, in this time, terrible to see what we do, terrible to be a woman, to know we birth such monsters. What would you be without women to suck the evil out of you? —

—We would destroy everything. —

—As you are doing now,— she said. —I don't see desire in you, Castle. Why did you ask me here? —

FOUR

Castle watched the flight attendants work. One of them was a tall, thin dark woman with a hawk nose. High cheekbones and clear black eyes said she was a highland Indian. The other was Nordic blond with blue eyes.

Castle approached the galley but stopped when he overheard the dark one—Genobeba was her name—repulsing an aggressive red-faced man.

—The nuns,— Genobeba said, —cautioned me against doing anything my aunts didn't teach me to do. And none of my aunts would ever do that. You should return to your seat and strap yourself in. —

Castle returned to his seat beside Everett who was sweating. His face flushed.

"Are you okay?" Castle said.

"God damn planes are too fucking hot," Everett said.

"Could have taken a private plane," Castle said.

"No. Can't do that."

Castle wondered why Everett hadn't sweated when they left New York.

"Look, Castle, when we land, I don't want the Aduana to open this briefcase so you know how to keep that from happening."

From his inside jacket pocket, Everett drew a packet of bills and handed it to Castle. His duties were becoming better defined the farther South they went. Everett had stopping talking in Miami. Now, as they approached Ayahuantu, Everett, like a lot of Americans let his xenophobia out. Castle knew how it worked—Americans either became loud and pushy or they retreated into small, tight corners of alienation and helplessness. That was Everett and Everett's sweat made more sense out of his situation. Castle tucked the packet of bills away. He said,

"They won't."

Everett panted like a dog. He said,

"You speak the lingo? Right?"

"I speak the lingo," Castle replied.

"That's why I brought you in, isn't it?"

******

From the air, Huañuscacuchu looked like a dead city. No red lights perched on hills, no beacons called attention to the buildings at the heart. Like fireflies a few flecks of light emerged from the void, lining the arteries that ran through the body.

Dawn broke its shell to spread light and the sky lost that intense mourning black that it carries in the altiplano as if the air had to sacrifice itself in order to give those few survivors breath.

Closer to the ground, pairs of headlights probed black streets—white stilettos piercing dark flesh.

******

Looking at them, Castle felt like a dead man watching maggots of some bizarre species of insect devour him.

Nacionales.

Everywhere.

Their white helmets protruded from their heads like round larvae.

Their uniforms—either pale or sickening green, tan, khaki—shimmered the shimmer of writhing grass.

—Tourists? —the inspector spoke.

Castle started. He had expected a dry rattling of mandibles instead of human speech. He had felt fear before. He knew the bite of the voice, the curl of the lip, the hate seething from the mouth. Glancing back at the Nacionales who cut their way through the crowd of descending passengers like knives through fresh meat, Castle shrugged off the dread and nodded yes. He set his suitcase on the inspection table.

The customs agent opened the battered valise and smiled. He said,

—This is all you bring? —

Castle looked at Everett so wet with sweat he glistened. His lips quavered, his face the bright red of a man who drank too much. Castle felt the two Nacionales approach and he sensed Everett's fear. Fear printed on him clear as words on a page and Castle expected to hear the footsteps crackle to a halt behind him. The briefcase. The briefcase was the root of Everett's anxiety. Or was it?

The Nacionales didn't stop because Everett was a gringo and gringos in Ayahuantu meant money.

—You must not anticipate a long stay in my country, sir. —

—I lost everything at the track in Miami,— Castle said.

—The track. You like the horses? —

His eyes downcast, he fingered a t-shirt.

—Dogs,— Castle said.

—Dogs? —

—Dogs. —

—My cousin has a friend in Buenos Aires. He has four horses. —

—Yes. The Argentines are fond of horses. —

—Horses are more expensive than dogs—. The inspector turned to Everett who was trembling, his breath coming in short gasps. Castle wanted to reach out to steady Everett, but he heard the boots pause, then walk past. The inspector had broken out in a light sweat. Castle knew that the inspector did not want Everett to collapse either. He did not want to share his cache with the Nacionales and if they stopped, if they opened the suitcase, they would find cash. Lots of it.

There was a peculiar odor to them as they passed by, an odor like the odor of decaying animal hair left buried and then unearthed. The inspector said,

—The big one, he is your father? —

—I am his companion,— Castle said. —He does not speak the language and he does not like the track although he never loses. He has come here to buy things. —

—In Ayahuantu, we have many goods to sell, but alas we have no track for horses or for dogs. —

He glanced at the Nacionales, now a few meters away, automatic weapons dangling from their shoulders like dark death-bolts, talking and lighting cigarettes, then at the briefcase Castle held in his left hand. He said,

—That is true and truly a pity because I would like to lose these awful shirts my brother-in-law gave me. —

The inspector smiled. Castle said,

—You seem to have dropped your notebook, Inspector. —

Castle slid one of Everett's suitcases to reveal a packet of bills. The inspector glanced from the bills back to the briefcase and then in the direction of the Nacionales. He said,

—You speak my language, well for a man traveling with a gringo.—

He retrieved the packet of money and inserted it into his notebook.

The Nacionales had turned away, trails of smoke following them, masking the odor of rotting flesh. Castle said,

—It is a beautiful language, Inspector. I read the newspapers. I go to the cinema and I have a Rosetta Stone that I carry with me. —

He patted the briefcase. The Inspector smiled and he relaxed. The Nacionales, reaching the end of the terminal, went outside.

The Inspector shoved Everett's unopened suitcases down the line. He turned to a woman waiting behind Everett. He said,

—Madam, it is good to see you again. You return so soon from Miami? How is your sister? —

—Not well, Inspector,— the woman said.

*****

Castle hustled Everett through the terminal and into a cab waiting at the curb. Everett collapsed. He was wet as though he had caught a rain storm.

Taking his seat beside the driver, Castle looked him in the eye and, as if he had known him his entire life, said,

—Good to see you, man. —

—Where to, brother? —

—You know the Centro de Comercio on Manco Capac? —

FIVE

Calle Manco Capac was a narrow street one block from the baroque cathedral on Independence Square. The street was bounded on both sides by long stone and iron buildings with balconies that dreamed of an old Huañuscacuchu.

On the façade of a colonial four story, in blue letters on a cracked white enamel plaque it said Centro de Comercio e Industria.

The building, a fusion of rock and iron, had the broken feel of masterworks from other centuries in a world that lives with no future in mind. The structure had withstood the foundation and extinction of an empire and time had eaten holes in it, holes that had forgotten how to cry out for help.

The sidewalk, a mosaic of cobblestones and shattered tile, looked like it been pieced together from the remains of sacked pagan temples.

In the awakening grays of predawn light, the rust stains on the stone gave off remembrances of blood seeping from wounds in the gray flesh of time. The iron, driven deep, had long ago found the beating heart of a broken world.

When the cab pulled away. Castle glanced at Everett, saw the last sheen of sweat from the encounter with the inspector at the airport. Everett said,

"Do you have to suck up to these people?"

"If it makes you uncomfortable…"

"First you and that maniac in Miami. Christ you acted like he was your brother and now this goon—like he knew you from kindergarten."

"It's what you pay me to do," Castle said. "To know what they're thinking, you have to become one of them."

"I don't like it when you act like a chameleon."

Castle followed the big man into the Centro. He said,

"People in Ayahuantu are troubled. The elections.."

"I know about elections," Everett said.

Inside the building, plants grew in an open atrium, their green a contrast to the stone and iron grown around them. A fountain in the center trickled a weak flutter. In the sun of the day, light would cascade in with a crispness that dreamed of a brook and forest. The Mozarabic architecture living its past had achieved a slim perfection that echoed an importance forgotten.

Footsteps echoing in the emptiness of the stairwell, Castle walked with Everett up the worn marble steps that turned out onto a gallery looking down on the fountain. The flagstones of the atrium were wet. Moss dressed the edges of the stone in a trim of funeral black crêpe.

Everett groped for a key in his jacket pocket. The unmarked door on the third floor yielded to Everett's key. The second he walked in Everett's manner changed. He loosened his tie, set the briefcase on a desk. The caustic resentment that had shaded him from New York to Huañuscacuchu was gone. For a moment, he was almost jovial. He nodded at a closed door.

"I'm going to be in there a while," he said. "When things finish up, I want you to rent us a car. American, not one of those fucking Asian tin boxes. Park on the street. And keep your eyes open. I'm going to leave here by three and I don't want to be seen. There's a back door. It's barred. Get here about two-fifty—you come in the front, let me know, and then go back and drive around. You know what to look for."

"What am I looking for?" Castle said.

"If they're on to you, you'll know."

Everett took a second key from his pocket, fingered it with a thoughtful look on his face, as if he didn't intend to open the inner door until Castle was gone.

"Okay," Castle said. "Two-fifty back here."

He reached the door just as Everett unlocked the office. Castle shut the door to the corridor. He heard the sharp expletive. He came back in to find Everett still in the entryway.

Castle smelled death. On the floor, in the dull light, the body of a woman.

She had not died fast. She lay twisted, lacerations to her face, a long gash just under the ribs on her right side, a gash made with a heavy blade—a sabre, or a machete.

A purse lay in a corner. Contents spilled on the floor. The handle of a small pistol protruded from the purse.

Castle knelt beside her. A small woman. Dark skinned. Ayahuantan. Chunks of flesh had lodged under her fingernails.

Castle inventoried the room. A small safe open. Reels of recording tape scattered. File cabinet ransacked. A small cassette recorder shattered against a wall.

It was no longer simple. Everett was now in the doorway. He said, "Don't presume."

"Who is she?"

"A secretary."

"What was in the safe?"

"Gold bullion."

"You want me to believe that?"

"You know what you need to know, Castle."

"Gold. You're paying someone off."

"What?"

"What they wanted wasn't in the safe so they hit the file cabinet."

"Astute, but not quite fact."

"What is fact, Everett? It's time you filled me in. There's a basic problem with your operation and I don't know what to do because I don't know why I'm here."

"She was killed because she discovered them cracking the safe."

"Why does Centrex operate out of here?"

"That doesn't matter to you."

"But someone knows and takes the gold."

"You're way off on this," Everett said.

"What's on the tapes?"

"It doesn't matter now."

"Call the Nacionales."

"Can't do that. It's like they're reading my mind."

"What's the project?" Castle said.

"You're a snippy little bastard, Castle. We're running out of time or I'd ship you back home but I have a meeting and what I'm doing is worth a few lives and they know it."

"They," Castle said. "Who are they?"

"Down here people are always disappearing."

"You want me to make all this disappear?" Castle said.

"I can't leave her, and I can't let the Nacionales in on it."

Castle knew that the smart thing was to walk out the door. He knew that if he left, Everett wouldn't stop him. He looked at the big man, the frown, the sweat, the huge wrinkled forehead, the green eyes. One thing he was sure of, no matter what Everett told him, it was miles from the truth. But a woman was dead, something valuable was missing, and Everett needed help.

SIX

The four Nacionales in the jeep patrolled Avenida de la Independencia on the west side of the plaza. With each pass in front of the café, patrons lowered their eyes to peer into the mystery hiding in their coffee cups.

The *quena* player sitting against the base of the statue of liberty playing an Incaica, paid them no attention. It was possible that he felt their passing just as a sensitive plant will cower in the wake of a large snake crawling.

The Nacionales were not interested in the café patrons, not even the one at a sidewalk table reading a day-old edition of La Voz Ayahuantina. There was nothing noteworthy about him. With his olive skin and black hair, he could have been Greek or Basque. He could have been Peruvian or Ayahuantan. It was possible to imagine him sitting in a café in Trebizond or running to catch a bus in Munich or even lifting bales on a ship docked in Dublin or Rio.

As Castle watched the Nacionales drive past the Ford convertible parked halfway down the street, he calculated the probability that they would find the body of the woman in the large suitcase in the trunk.

*****

When he traveled, Castle carried only what he needed. Once in place, he bought his camouflage—a cotton jacket that was not new, a pair of boots with scuffed toes, a tan shirt with twin breast pockets stained with ink—and the suitcase. Seeing him, you would have thought he was Ayahuantuan and the more he sank into the air of Huañuscacuchu, the more he melded into it. In his ease, he read the fear in the eyes and rounded shoulders of the café patrons. The tourists who wandered off the path of ruins and craft shops were blind to the tension.

Ayahuantuans knew. They pretended that if they saw nothing, nothing could happen to them. If they saw the Nacionales make an arrest, they said nothing. If they saw a rebel beaten in the street, they did not protest. Driving their blindness was the man who designed the tactics the Nacionales used. To control the men, the Nacionales arrested the women. To control the women, the Nacionales abducted children. If a Nacionale sprayed bullets into a crowd, the man who wrote the rules would apologize for the accident. The man who wrote the rules had studied history, knew history, knew the power of random violence and the power of the sudden disappearance. It was the complete vanishing that grew the horror and the Ayahuantuans remained quiet and anonymous. The man who wrote the rules was a master controlling the tools of political manipulation.

Elections. Castle glanced at La Voz in front of him. An election was coming, but you would not know it from the news in La Voz. Knowing how to read what was left out was a skill, and without it, you could not see the total bankruptcy of a once honest press.

Castle understood what he was seeing. He had seen it in other countries. He understood anonymity and the cultivated practice of being nothing. He knew that men such as he had existed for as long as there had been secrecy. He knew that he had to move in silence while hearing everything, but never be noticed. He knew that he had to become the color of the atmosphere. He folded La Voz and looked at the Nacionales as they stopped beside the Ford convertible with the woman in the suitcase in the trunk. They were relaxed, not searching for anyone, not making arrests. Castle returned to the newspaper.

On an inside page, maybe an editorial afterthought, under a photograph of a man in full military uniform but without definite rank badges, was an article about

Alfredo Vargas. Vargas was Chief of the Policia Nacional, Minister of Internal Security, and the de facto ruler of Ayahuantu.

In any other newspaper, in any other country such articles about public figures were routine but in Ayahuantu it was a special event if you knew how to read it. Vargas preferred to remain dark, talked about but never seen. His existence had a mythical bent to it. That he was there, on the page, photographed and written about was so unusual that it could only mean something important was going to take place.

Castle read the article deeper the second time, letting the words flow into his mind, trying to peel away the meanings from the statements. The Minister, the article said, had just returned from a trip abroad. The phrase—abroad—was so indefinite that Castle wondered why it was mentioned. He had consulted with industrialists and had given them assurances that there would never be any political violence in Ayahuantu.

Political violence. Fifteen years before, when, an ambitious colonel, he became head of state, the Nacionales were a personal instrument he used to direct political life. The only violence would be by the Nacionales.

Castle knew it was strange Varga had mentioned it in his interview. Letting the words percolate through his brain, Castle came to the end of his computation.

The Nacionales left the Ford with the dead woman in the trunk.

Everett? No. He wasn't an industrialist. He was scared of the Nacionales. If he were an important foreigner, he would have carte blanche. Instead, he acted like the avant-garde of a commando unit.

On the last page of the paper there was an article announcing a reading by Federico Talavera, one of the rising suns of poetry. Castle was puzzled. He knew the political leanings of Talavera, a student of the infamous author of *Veinte poemas de amor y una canción desdichada.* It surprised Castle to see the notice of a reading instead of a notice of Talavera's arrest.

Glancing at his watch, Castle finished his coffee, folder the paper, and counted change into a saucer.

The *quena* player still sat under the statue.

Castle got to his feet, timing his exit from the café with the passing of two young women.

Shoulders moving with the provocative sway that Ayahuantuan women mastered at the age of six, they undulated past.

Castle skittered across the square using the bacchanalian parade as cover. On his way to the Ford with the dead women in the trunk, he dropped coins in the lap of the *quena* player as compensation for the miracle he was missing.

At 2:50, Castle pulled up at the entrance to the hotel, ran upstairs to the door and knocked then hustled back down and drove around to the alley behind the building where he waited for Everett. Wearing dark glasses and carrying the briefcase, Everett sat in the seat beside Castle.

Castle drove away. He said,

"The Nacionales are out."

"What are they doing?"

"Vargas has returned," Castle said.

Everett adjusted his dark glasses and cleared his throat.

SEVEN

Two kilometers out of Huañuscacuchu, Castle left the pavement. Maguey plants on the top of the high stone fences sliced the sky with their fanged blades.

An hour outside the capital, Castle slowed. Everett said,

"What're you doing?"

Castle shut the Ford down and got out. He walked behind the car and stood looking around. No trails of dust. Nobody trudging across the llano.

It was silent.

No wind.

Complete silence.

Everett got closed the door as he exited the car. He stood back, watching Castle.

Castle opened the trunk. Tugged the suitcase up on the lip of the trunk and let it tumble to the ground. Everett said,

"For Christ's sake. What are you doing?"

The body of the woman rolled out into the dust.

Castle had stripped off her clothes, her jewelry. Thrown them away.

The purse he had tossed into the sewer.

The money he had given to the *quena* player.

All that remained was the naked, headless torso.

"What the fuck," Everett said.

Castle picked up the head. He tucked the head under this arm.

"You fucking animal," Everett said.

"The head wouldn't fit in the suitcase with the body. They'd almost done it. I finished it."

"She was in this car all the time?" Everett said.

"I didn't want to leave her in the city," Castle said.

"This little detour throws a monkey wrench into my plans."

"You wanted her gone," Castle said,

"I said get rid of her, but I expected you to be more professional."

"I'll get you to Tarma tonight," Castle said. "Give me a hand. I don't want to drag her."

Everett gagged as he grasped the dead woman's ankles. He turned his head. He said,

"I can't."

He dropped the legs. The sudden release jerked the torso from Castle's grasp.

"At least wrap her in a blanket," Everett said.

"Don't have a blanket."

"I can't."

"All right."

Castle pitched the head away from the body, then grasping the corpse by the heels, he dragged her across the field then stopped to move the head. When he was a hundred meters from the car, he held up, laid the body out, placed the head on the chest and piled stones on it. The head on the body, the mutilated breasts now covered in dust, lips peeled back over the teeth. Castle worked until she disappeared under the heaped stones.

*****

Access to Tarma was through cuts in the rock of a formidable mountain that towered above the gorge where water rushed seaward in a white foam. Tarma was a haven reserved for kings, but now it gave itself and its secrets to the automobile.

Once through the mountain, the road opened to a vista of a crystalline-blue lake that covered much of the valley like a mirror reflecting the snow-capped peaks—extinct volcanos— and the deep aquamarine sky.

Steep terraces marked the hillsides in a mosaic of planted plots—all the work of farmers who understood the rigors of high mountain crops.

Vicuñas and guanacos roamed the valley, the offspring of animals brought there by the sun-kings centuries ago. Tarma had outlasted the rulers of the four Suyus, it had lived past the gold-hungry conquerors who changed the names the Indians used to identify their world. The conquerors had taken the gold and the silver and had added only misery, wheels, wheat, and iron while they had left the ancient agrarian methods that had domesticated the *pallar*, groomed the teosinte from a wild seed into a multicolored staple, and tamed the *papa* throughout the altiplano.

In the twilight, Castle drove on a stone road that had been laid down hundreds of years before Charles V dreamed of the empire that later became the domain of United Fruit and the Copper Corporation.

Rounding the shore of the lake, they approached a small hotel nestled in the timelessness of the mountains. Built on a stone foundation, the hotel was a jewel set by the lake and unaware of its own history.

The sun sank beyond the pinnacles. Shadows darkened to blues and deep purples while the yellow of the fields took on a rich, dark gold. The colors were history itself—after the rulers of Tahuantinsuyu came the viceroys and after the viceroys came the presidents and after the presidents came the generals who saw themselves as the ordained violators of the people as they disavowed their heritage by stealing all the gold they could carry, leaving the people no choice but to toss them onto the middens of history.

The air turned chilly. Castle slowed. Ahead, he saw the flecks of green and white growing larger. A tightening in his chest. He glanced at Everett. Calm.

Castle shut down the engine. In the crisp, thin air, fumes hung with the putridity of carcasses forgotten in a slaughterhouse. Everett looked up. A nod.

Perched like a species of green and white vulture, a contingent of Nacionales guarded the entrance to the hotel. As Everett stepped out of the Ford, and to Castle's surprise, the Nacionales snapped to attention, automatic weapons at present arms, saluting. Castle glanced again at Everett who, exiting the car, stretched, yawned, paying no attention to the troops as though he expected them to be there. Castle imagined burying the woman under her mortuary stones while Everett looked away. And now? Nothing. No fear. No sweat.

It didn't fit. A small man ran out of the ornate, carved doorway through the still saluting Nacionales.

He bowed to Everett and called him by name.

He smiled at Castle, introduced himself as Onorato, majordomo.

Castle noticed his Spanish was thick, accented with the Ayahuantuan dialect.

Then, with the flair of a trained commander, he ordered the Nacionales to bring in the luggage.

Automatonlike, the Nacionales slung their weapons over their shoulder.

Everett handed the briefcase the Castle.

The Nacionales carried the small bags and the empty suitcase into the hotel.

Up a flight of baroque marble stairs, and at Onorato's command, the Nacionales set the luggage down outside a carved door. Onorato dismissed them. Castle admired his military manners.

The Nacionales saluted, clicked their heels, and disappeared down the stairway.

Onorato opened the door for Everett.

Onorato carried the suitcases into the room.

Everett took the briefcase from Castle. He said,

"You go with him. We'll go down in half an hour. I want to talk to you before that."

Everett's manner had changed from fearful to secure.

Castle understood. The hotel was home turf. Somehow. That didn't register as right.

Everett closed the door when Castle followed Onorato into the corridor.

—Have you worked here long, Onorato? —

Onorato glanced at him, no surprise.

He opened a door, drew the drapes. He turned down the opulent bed. He said,

—No, señor, I do not work here. —

Castle was pleased. Sometimes for fear of ridicule, Indians did not reply in kind.

—We come with Don Eduardo. —

—But you are the majordomo. —

—Yes, sir. Here and in Huañuscacuchu. —

Castle pulled back the drapes, peered down at the Nacionales who had retaken their vigilance at the entry to the hotel.

—We? —Castle said. –You and the Nacionales? —

—No, señor. They come only when we leave the city. There are three of us. Tiyuca and I and Doña Marta. There are others in the city. Don Eduardo...—

—Who is Don Eduardo? —Castle said.

Onorato looked at him, eye to eye, no fear in him, no subservience. Castle sensed a man of many talents, one of which was to disguise all emotion.

—The patron. —

—He lives here? —

"No, señor, in the city. In the big house. —

—You mean Huañuscacuchu? —

—Yes, señor. —

—I don't want you to call me señor, — Castle said.

Onorato shuffled his feet, did not look away. But he hesitated.

—Are there other guests in this hotel? —

—Just you and señor Everett. —

—My name is Castle. I'm a servant to Everett. There can be no formality between servants. —

Onorato looked down. When he looked up, the liquid black eyes, the high cheekbones and eagle nose were the perfect and proud picture of the Indians who had built Tarma. He said,

—A servant perhaps, but no ordinary servant. You speak my language, the language of a conquered people without shame or hesitation. Not even señorita Gloria had that facility. —

—Who is Gloria? —

—She came with Don Everett, just as you have now come. —

—He has been here many times? —

—Many times? No. —

—This Gloria. Was she always with him when he came? —

—No…Castle, there were others before her. Don Everett has had many assistants. —

—He is a harsh patron, Onorato. Others could not take it. —

—You can take much, can you not, Castle? Perhaps we have talked too long. — Onorato shuffled his feet. Castle read him. He said,

—Of course. You have work. Let no one know, Onorato. A secret. —

—So it shall be. This skill is a shame for many, meaningless to others. —

Castle clasped Onorato by the shoulder. The majordomo stepped out into the corridor. Castle went to the window. The Nacionales were still in their places.

Gloria. Gloria was the dead woman in the office. The dead woman he had buried. What had happened in the office? What did Everett have in that briefcase?

*****

Castle knocked on Everett's door. He entered. Everett leaned over the escritoire and closed the notebook there. He dropped it into the briefcase. He looked business-like—white shirt, tie, black suit, black shoes. The snap had returned to his voice. There was a sharp edge to his movements that made Castle think of broken glass. Everett said,

"We're going down to talk to Eduardo Villareal. I don't want them to know you speak the language, so sit there and look stupid."

"Them?" Castle said.

Villareal. He knew the name Villareal. Onorato's Don Eduardo was Eduardo Villareal. A name written in the history of Ayahuantu. The Patron.

"He has a woman who talks for him. Don't do anything to tip our hand because she's a hellcat who could tear off a man's nuts in two seconds flat."

"I'll watch myself," Castle said.

"I don't know how she got her hooks into Villareal, but she's sharp. I've worked around her before so watch your Ps and Qs."

Everett fussed with his tie. Patted his handkerchief in place. He looked ready.

"Does Villareal speak English?" Castle said.

"Can't tell. Either he's faking it or he's too god-damned lazy to learn or he can't be bothered. You might be able to tell. You read their eyes, right?"

"Maybe."

"Anyhoo, he's that way. Doesn't have a lot of respect for your American businessman and that's the kind I like to skin alive. You know, Castle, I'm learning something about this language shit. I used to think it was better not to speak it at all, but now I think that if I did, I could think while they're talking and still talk through an interpreter. Have a leg up then. Negotiations take longer because you have to say everything twice."

"Do I need to be briefed on what you're negotiating?"

"No. You'll figure it out. When we leave here I want you to get rid of that big suitcase. Should have dumped it a long time ago. Briefcase. Your third arm. That's why you're here—to hold onto that briefcase. All right, my short-peckered friend, let's go give'em hell."

*****

Villareal's interpreter dressed in black. She had the executive style of a shark. Castle dug under her words and he found that this wasn't an interpreter working between worlds, this was a woman who possessed the words and shared them with reluctant gluttony. She spoke to Everett as an equal, told Villareal what to do, and ignored Castle as though he were a piece of furniture in need of polish.

The hard streak was counterpointed by her tendency to lead with her breasts. Placing her arms on the table and leaning forward, she swelled her breasts so they rolled when she talked. Because she was thin, her breasts appeared large and complex. Everett was stricken, Villareal looked sleepy.

She had bleached her hair stark white while the rest of her skin was a sun-deprived pallor balanced by a reliance on cosmetics that gave her a startling and surreal beauty. Everett was captivated. Villareal ignored her as he examined his fingernails.

The breasts. A negotiating weapon so entrancing that a man seeing so much skin failed to take her seriously. Castle did not dismiss her. He knew danger when he saw it, knew power when it spilled out with the energy of an earthquake.

She spoke perfect English with no national accent. Not even a hidden vowel or a liquid in place of a lateral. Where was she from? Castle closed his eyes to let her words settle into his brain. He turned them over-- meat on a spit, feeling the sounds the way some men feel thighs and lips so that the words possessed a physical sexuality.

When he opened his eyes, Castle knew a great deal about her. The sharpness was the cutting edge of a woman who knew men and their weaknesses. A woman who used men as if they were disposable inserts to be used then flushed away. Castle shuddered with loathing, anticipation, sensing in her more than a small portion of himself.

No, this was not an interpreter. She was part of Villareal. She spoke his language as if she were in his mind.

The problem this woman presented to Castle was how to mask a lust that she would feel with the ease of a seismograph tracking a tectonic event in Chile. The mask he chose was the blank look that could be mistaken for the empty mind of a

25

stupid man. Castle did it well. He congratulated himself on doing it well. He looked at Villareal as if in reading him, he could read Marta as well.

Villareal was an emaciated man so thin that when he turned sideways, he disappeared like some creature out of flatland. There was a sullen air of depravity that masked him the way fog masks a lake. He wore dark glasses in the dim lamp light. A pointed beard at the tip of a weak chin emphasized his trembling lips. Limp, quivering white hands tipped with long and perfect nails gave the illusion that he was holding a bar of mushy warm soap. Castle knew that Villareal's presence at the table was a perfunctory stop lasting long enough for him to eat dinner before selling out what remained of his principles, before returning to the debauch.

Eduardo Villareal was not a man who had charted a redemptive course for his life. He made a mess of his place at the dinner table. He missed what he was stabbing at with his fork. He smeared juice and grease on the cloth.

His weaknesses were many. Yet this scion of a decaying nobility possessed a sense of humor rooted in an infantile and surreal wit that is the signature of an undernourished intelligence.

Everett pretended not to notice the idiosyncrasies of Villareal. He chatted with a relaxed grace about the trip south, about the stock market, about the role of Ayahuantu in the world economy, and state-side politics. But Villareal was a man bored with grace and charm. He yawned and picked at his elegant fingernails as Marta translated Everett's remarks, and he made occasional comments that Marta, while watching Everett, did not translate.

Castle continued to show his stupid side while studying the interplay. He realized that Everett was acting. The grace and charm were traits of the character he was playing—the American businessman working his customers. He knew when to strike and when to hold out a velvet glove. The target was fixed in his sights and now he was selling. Selling and buying at the same time. Castle knew that. He did not know what the stakes were.

*****

After dinner, Castle sat back, his mind working like a razor on the intonations, seeking more than meaning, trying to squeeze intention out of the core thought. The discussion was quick, mercurial, intense.

His eyelids sagging, Castle felt Villareal under the words while Marta edited those words. He became uncomfortable. He looked at Everett. Everett showed nothing, didn't respond to the contradictions spewing out of Villareal's mouth.

Nothing on paper. Nothing finalized. Castle knew this was one in a series of negotiations regarding what, he did not know because they spoke in a verbal shorthand, that bureaucratic acronym salad that baffled everyone but initiates and linguists.

Marta, after a short aside to Villareal turned to Everett and said,

"Don Eduardo says that if the rights must be granted in perpetuity, you must increase the initial payment. And you must increase the guarantee. It must be off the gross exports and payable in five-year lump sums based on your projections not the actual amounts."

Everett sat looking at them. Castle wasn't there. Everett cleared his throat. Sweat popped up on his enormous forehead. He took a deep breath. He said,

"Tell Don Eduardo that this is not a business proposal. What he suggests is not only impossible, it is a joke."

Marta whispered. Villareal nodded. Marta said,

"It is not a joke."

"It is a one eighty from his previous position."

"Yes it is."

"We had an agreement. Now we don't. Why do you want to revisit this question?"

Marta said, "Don Eduardo asks why he should subsidize your operation."

"An advance of that magnitude isn't possible. And on the gross? Who can do business that way?"

Marta said, "Don Eduardo says that yours is not the only way."

"What if the quality of the material decreases?" Everett said.

—Are you a gambler? —Don Eduardo said. Castle looked at the smiling face.

"What did he say?" Everett snapped.

Marta said, "He asked if you are a gambler."

"We are left paying for tonnage that doesn't yield. No, Mr. Villareal," Everett said. "A one-year advance. On the net."

—I have no control over your accounting methods, — Don Eduardo said.

"What did he say?"

Marta said, "He has only the word of your accounts that the tallies are right."

"Do you suspect us of cheating you?"

—We have been cheated for centuries, —Don Eduardo said.

Marta said, "It has happened." Castle glanced at her, she ignored him.

"We don't do business that way. We honor our contracts."

Marta said, —He won't change. It is his way. —

—As it always is with the gringos, — Don Eduardo said. —Tell him to go fuck himself. —

"What did he say?" Everett was bright red and sweating.

Marta said, "Don Eduardo repeats that those are the new conditions."

"That's not what he said."

"Those are the conditions and, of course, we have options."

"What options?"

Villareal sat shaking his head, sipping crème de menthe from a long-stemmed glass. He leaned close to Marta and whispered. Castle listened. Villareal said,

—Tell him the Russians will meet our conditions for the mineral. —

Marta said, "You have to risk at the same level he does, Mr. Everett. And you know what he is risking."

"Good god, man." Everett spat as he exploded. "I know what he's risking but what company can meet those conditions and still..."

"Make a profit?" Don Eduardo said.

"You do speak English, you little shit," Everett said.

Castle leaned close. Laid his hand on Everett and shook his head.

—I'm weary, Marta. Why do they send whales to toy with us? I need to lie down. Dinner is making me ill, or perhaps it is this fat pig. —

"Have him tell me that in English," Everett said.

"Don Eduardo doesn't understand why you equivocate," Marta said.

"I'm not equivocating. He speaks English, why doesn't he say it in English?"

—Tell this idiot that I have seen burros with more brains. —

"What did he say?" Everett shouted.

Marta said, "Don Eduardo asks if you need time to consider the revised proposition."

"I'll have to consult with headquarters," Everett said. "That'll take time."

—Ask the bald one if he thinks his anglo company is the only company after what we have. —

"Don Eduardo feels that this discussion can go no farther until you have spoken with your superiors," Marta said.

—Perhaps we can meet in Huañuscacuchu in two days unless this whale dies a sudden death. —

Villareal got up from the table and with a yawn, made his way out of the dining room.

"You don't have to tell me," Everett said. "I heard Huañuscacuchu in there. Another rendezvous. Shit. Fucking spicks always mañana."

Marta followed Villareal out, leaving Castle and Everett in a room full of wrought iron and carved walnut furniture.

"What the fuck is going on, Castle?"

Castle summed up the conversation leaving out Villareal's comments.

Everett, nodding, said,

"So the Russians are dipping their wick in this honeypot."

"Sounds that way."

"Was she honest?"

"She translated most of what he said."

"And that means we're fucked."

"That's how it feels," Castle said. "This woman isn't just a translator though. She's the stronger of the two. In a street fight, she wins. She controls things."

Everett, on his feet, patrolled the room. He said,

"That's damned interesting, Castle."

Everett stopped his tour of the room. He eyed Castle, his forehead sopping. He said,

"You handled yourself all right, Castle. That gives me a little more faith in my judgement. You can go now."

"I wonder if you're going about this the right way."

"As in?"

"They do things differently down here. Time and pace are different."

"Well you tell me what that little fuck wants."

"There are the words," Castle said, "and then there's something else coming through—down in there in that screwed up skull, there's something like a nationalist."

"A commie?"

"No. Not that. It's not political."

"What is it?"

"They're not going to give you want you want."

"They all talk money no matter what the language is."

"It's not just money," Castle said. "The days are gone when Americans came down here and ran over these people. Evo Morales set the tone, now…"

"You're right," Everett said. "You're talking colonialism. Well I'm not talking colonialism. It's a sin to be a businessman now, you know that, right? Look what we've given the world and look what we get in return. These little cocksuckers call profits disease but they can't wait to suck it up. It's not all on us, Castle. It used to be we just had to buy and sell things. But times changed, you're fucking well right and now we have to buy people. Yeah, times have changed again and this time we're talking about buying a whole fucking country."

Everett sat back down. He studied Castle. He said,

"You know these people, you know their language, but can you respect people who've been sitting here all these years while there was money in the ground? We're businessmen. We come down here to do business, we don't come down here to underwrite social progress. If we're not buying the caciques, we're paying off the bleeding-heart commie shits who want to take social progress out of our profits.

"This Villareal and that slut he's hammering—how long as he been here? That son of a bitch keeps slaves. You know that? Slaves. He doesn't give a damn about people as long as he gets what he thinks we'll give him and if he doesn't get it from us, he'll go somewhere else. We'll pull their future out of the ground that's for sure and if they want social progress, let the Villareals pay for it. A company has the obligation to run at a profit. We come along with our know-how, our money and show them how to make a go of it and they whine that we're taking advantage of them. We build the fucking country and they want to kick us out on our butts. Well, it's happened before, but it sure as dick ain't gonna happen this time. No little pseudo-prince who sits in his mountain kingdom with his finger up his ass is gonna hi-jack us. We don't have to care what he wants, by god, we'll just take it. Good night, Castle. Catch a few zs, 'cause we're driving back early."

EIGHT

Castle was not comfortable. The opulence of living in a work of art irked him. He did not belong. He was there by circumstance not by choice.

He studied the paneling of the baroque ceiling. In each corner, surrounded by florid eighteenth-century pastoral painting, were portraits of pairs of cherubim. Though their sex was obscured, one of each pair was Eros poised with his bow, arrow nocked, while the other was a nubile female—twisted in that dynamic pose on one knee, back to the viewer, rounded buttocks resembling breasts pressed together—who reminded him of Marta, the enigmatic, pneumatic Marta of the white hair, Marta who gave orders to Onorato, a majordomo who gave orders to the Nacionales, Nacionales—men of vicious cruelty, who obeyed him like marionettes. Fear. Shame. Guilt.

Some people see the virgin in their morning toast. Others discover hideous details of their tortured childhoods in ink spots. Castle did not see anything in the cherubim in the corners of the room, but the cherubim made him think of Marta and the Nacionales and how they related to Everett.

None of it figured. He had buried a nameless woman in an unmarked grave. He had come to a meeting that Everett had said was pivotal, but it had been cancelled in half an hour.

Enigmatic Marta. Puzzling Nacionales. Marta stood at the heart of the thing.

Castle understood the nature of capital and how to manage it, but he thought little about money either as a medium of exchange or as power base.

He saw the world in terms of action and women.

Action he understood because it meant conflict.

With women, he no longer, as he had in his rutting days, thought with the head of his penis rather now he thought with the brain in his head.

Uncomfortable with the opulence, tired of the cherubim, he got off the bed and went downstairs. Wending through dark corridors, he came to the kitchen where Onorato sat at a plain wooden table eating. He said,

—You can't sleep, Castle?
—All that gold gives me the fever, — Castle said.
—Yes, there is much gold. —
Castle pulled a wooden chair, strung with llama hide, away from the table. He sat. He said,
—You work late and hard, Onorato. —
—There is hot water if you will have Ovaltina. —
—That is for nurses and small children, —Castle said. –I need aguardiente. —
—For that we need a tavern, but in Tarma, there is the lake full of water. —
—Beer then? —Castle said.
He got up and rummaged through a cupboard, came up with a bottle of Cristal. He poured two glasses of beer. He said,
—Don Eduardo, does he come here often? —
–When the tourists have gone. —
—Does he always bring the lady with him? —
—The fox smells a chicken. —
—She interests me, Onorato. Gloria, for example, she interests me but I do not know her. —
—Gloria, yes. —
—Is she Ayahuantuana? —
—I think not. Perhaps guatemalteca. —
—Why do you think that? —
—She once told me she has a cousin there. But she has cousins in many places. Castle, she is not like other women. —
—How is she different? —
—In many ways. —
—How tall is she? —
—She is not tall. —
—Does she dress like a gringa? —
—What are you asking, Castle? —
—When did you last see her? —
—When she was last here. —
—Does Don Eduardo always bring the Nacionales? —
—Nacionales. —
—Is he in danger? —
—This I do not know. But when they are here they are like small children. —
Castle leaned on the table. He said,
—This is an excellent beer. —
—Yes. —
—Why come here, Onorato? —

—Perhaps because Tarma is isolated. It is a good place for Don Eduardo when he needs quiet. He is a very nervous man. —

—Is he ill? Perhaps his blood is thin. Or is it the nervousness of a man who abuses himself? —

—Don Eduardo comes here sometimes with women he has found in the city. You ask many questions, Castle. —

—I am an ignorant man. How do I end ignorance if I do not ask questions? —

—Yes. You are right. It is good to ask questions. —

—Why come here then? Why have this as a meeting place? —

—It is a good place here to meet the other *wiracochas*. —

Castle coughed and strangled on his beer laughing at Onorato's use of the insult. He said,

—You use a word I haven't heard since the last time I saw two gringos bargaining for a palta with an old lady in the plaza. It pains me that you don't trust me. —

Onorato looked at Castle, eye to eye, not blinking. Castle liked the penetrating stare. Onorato said,

—You know much for an ignorant man. —

—That is because I am a fool whose questions are sometimes answered. If they are not, I am so much a fool that I continue to ask them. Even a fool can learn if he listens to wise men when they speak. Which other *gentlemen* come here with Don Eduardo? —

—I do not know them by name. —

—But they come here, they talk to Don Eduardo, as Don Everett has done. What do they talk about? Do they talk about important things? —

—I know little of important things, Castle. —

—I mean him no harm,— Castle said. —It is for me that I ask because I am a very small cat in a very large room. I am curious. I do not talk to anyone about what I know. I respect your privilege, I respect your patron. I would not ask you to betray him. —

—The men who come, they are gringos like your patron but I do not know them by name. —

—Only lost children have no name and they soon die. —

—True. They must have names. We all have names or we could not pay taxes. But they are secretive, Castle. They talk to Don Eduardo just as you and Don Everett do, but they do not talk to me and I do not listen to them. —

—I talk to you, and you listen to me,— Castle said. —You talk to me because you are a man, because you have much to tell me. These men, when do they come?—

—They come at night. You arrive by day. You wear the *ushuta*, they wear boots. But they are not Nacionales. —

—Do they talk about the land, Onorato? —

—They talk about many things that I do not understand. I know very little, unlike you, Castle. I hear them when they think I am not there, but I do not understand what they say. There is much that bothers me. —

Onorato fell silent. He raised his head, his eyes darting to Castle's. He became a stone. His was the haunted demeanor of the Indian in the presence of death.

Out of the corner of his eye, Castle caught movement, movement of a pale vision as Marta entered the room.

She wore a black peignoir with a red feather boa. She wore black mules with tufts of feather on the toes. Castle came to his feet. She smiled. Onorato rose, shoulders arched under centuries of servitude. She ignored Onorato

"You are here," Marta said in English..

"I came for beer."

Marta turned to Onorato. She said,

—Don Eduardo isn't feeling well. Go to him now. —

Onorato bowed and was gone.

Marta used her eyes on Castle as if her eyes were a cat 'o nine tails.

And Castle felt like a man about to be whipped. He swallowed, tasting her perfume. Her eyes widened. She flared her nostrils and licked her scarlet lips. She said,

"If you wanted conversation, you should have come to me."

"Beer and glass," Castle said, "the sum of our conversation.

"Not very exciting."

"No, it was not."

"You were not in your room."

"You were looking for me?"

"Tiyuca said you were here. Why waste your time with an Indian when you can be with me? Come."

She slipped through the doorway, the peignoir a swirl of black.

Castle followed her to an open door. A large chair sat in front of a table lit by a single lamp. Spread on the table was a deck of tarot cards. An ashtray overflowed with half-smoked cigarettes. A brandy decanter—empty. Chance and Bacchus working in tandem.

His ego shrank to a pinpoint. He understood. It was not his animal magnetism that had brought her to him.

She stood at the foot of a canopied bed.

The flamboyant ceiling—color, action—did not conceal the intentions of the erotic baroque paintings that infused the room with an exotic energy.

Marta dropped the boa on the bed. The peignoir clung to her.

Castle let the waves of desire roll over him.

Her challenge aroused him.

To leave? To stay?

He knew that to her he was not a human, but a young bull—a living dildo, a warm mouthed orgasm machine.

He had seen it before, in other times, with other women.

She would possess him and he would be possessed.

She opened the drawer of a nightstand, a nightstand carved with glyphs Castle did not know.

She held out a grotesque mask with alien features. She said,

"Put this on."

Castle put it on. It smelled of latex and body powder. It smelled of perfume and sweat. The aroma of arousal had invaded its pores.

"Pull off my peignoir," she said.

She raised her arms. Castle, wearing the mask, slipped the peignoir from her shoulders. He touched her blazing white hair and smelled her body in the silk of the peignoir.

Naked, she sat on the edge of the bed and drew an enormous dong from the nightstand. Greenish. Gaudy purple. In the apparatus, he saw four ovoid shapes bulging like prey in the belly of a snake.

She handed him the phallus.

She lay back against the headboard and opened her legs. She said,

"Insert it."

Castle knelt. She quaked as he pressed the alien phallus against her skin.

She looked at him, her mouth open, her hips raised. She said, as if reading his mind,

"Yes. In."

The phallus slid into her and she screamed. She did not close her eyes but watched his gestures. She said, still in full voice,

"Squeeze."

Castle grasped the first egg and squeezed, moving the egg through the phallus and then, as he squeezed the second egg, Marta, her voice rasping, orgasmed. She hooked her heels around Castle's waist and said,

"Again."

Again Castle squeezed the egg through the phallus' opening mouth and again Marta orgasmed until the four eggs were in her.

Castle pulled away.

Looked at her face. Flushed. Sweaty. She said, her voice pulsating,

"What planet are you from?"

Castle watched her close her legs and watched her orgasms, the raised hips, listened to her grunting. She whispered,

"Tell me this is what you do to females on your home planet."

Opening her legs, she slid a pillow under her hips. She squeezed until the eggs slipped from her, one after the other. Each egg had a rough skin, a reptilian skin, a greenish, rough, sandpapery skin and as the eggs emerged from her, she muttered,

"Oh god, god, look at what you gave me."

She then sat up and nested the eggs in the silk sheet. She pulled the mask from Castle and set it beside the eggs on the sheet. She slipped on the black peignoir and then she glanced up at him and flicked a finger at him and she said,

"Go."

NINE

At eleven o'clock, Castle, naked, fell face first onto the bed. His eyes closed with fatigue but his brain kept churning—

The woman in black.

The mask.

The eggs.

She had him wondering who and what he was. He heard a knock on Everett's door.

He heard Everett's chair move.

A thump from Everett's room made Castle raise his head.

The Cordoba was no luxury hotel but thumping at midnight wasn't a good sign.

Castle heard a grunt, a thud, something hitting the wall. He was on his feet. He wrapped a towel around himself and ran into the corridor, pushed at Everett's half open door to see Everett staggering backwards, a shocked look on his face, his shirt ripped.

Coming at Castle, a large knife in hand, a dark man with a cold look in his eyes lunging.

Castle tore the towel from his waist and using it like a flail, cracked it in the man's eyes. The arm with the knife came up. A howl of pain as the man's hand rose to the injured eye. Castle cracked his arm and hit him in the bridge of the nose with the palm of his free hand, but the blow landed off target, the bone didn't break.

The knife clattered to the floor.

Scooping it up, Castle whirled as he caught, behind him, a second man carrying something very large. Castle brought the towel up as a shield and he felt the knife penetrate flesh, nicking bone, and there came a second, guttural growl.

And then they were gone.

Castle watched Everett collapse, tugging at the blade planted in his chest, the handle angled down. Everett looked up at Castle. His eyes squinted. Castle knelt. Everett blinked. His head sagged to his chest.

Castle ran into the hallway.

The lights feeding the darkness were two blurred yellow strips. Castle heard footsteps. A door closed.

Silence.

Back in the room, Castle saw that Everett had dragged himself across the floor.

He hung slumped over the desk.

His eyes glassy.

He was dead.

Castle closed the door. No sounds as if the hotel had emptied itself leaving only the dank smell of a dead man. Castle remembered the woman. The world had not been silent then.

The knife in his hand was a karambit, curved, claw-like, a gruesome weapon.

Castle glanced again at Everett. Face down on the desk in the room in the hotel, his right hand half-covered a stained sheet of paper.

On it were a name, an address, and one word—book.

Castle scanned the room for the briefcase. The black and silver case had become part of him and without it he felt that that part of him had been amputated.

He went to the bed. Lifted the mattress. Nothing.

The closet. Empty.

He searched the room. The briefcase was gone.

On the paper in his hand Castle read the name—Cathay. What book? Even dying, Everett refused to tell him the secrets.

Cathay. Book.

Back to the body, Castle leaned over, heard sounds. In the silence of the death-room, the ticking of Everett's watch hammered against the wood of the desk. Castle moved the big man. Everett slumped to the floor.

The notebook. That was the job—take the notebook to Cathay.

In Tarma, Castle had glimpsed one of the pages ripe with Everett's writing before he had closed the notebook and slipped it into the briefcase. The briefcase. Everett would have dropped the notebook there.

But where?

Everett was cautious. Like a miser with gold, he would have hoarded it. The knock had come on the door. Everett would have put the book away. It had to be in the briefcase.

Or in the desk.

He slid open the middle drawer.

There it was. The notebook.

The notebook was a fancy piece, a special binder. A combination lock. Sturdy locking straps. The heavy cover was made of a blue micarta. Tough.

Backtracking, Castle imagined the attack. One man struggled with Everett before planting the blade. The other had grabbed the briefcase. They hadn't expected Castle.

He felt cold.

He was sweating.

He realized that he had the notebook and that the lock strap was loose.

He snapped the lock.

It was instinctual like lying to authorities.

He locked it because Everett always locked it.

He knew death.

Death was as natural to him as sunlight. Death neither frightened him nor elated him. Death meant nothing once the reaction to danger had passed.

He had to do something. A normal human might first have thought of the police. It was, in fact, the most remote act imaginable. At that second, steeped in the smell of death, Castle was spurred on by survival. What did he do without Everett? Did he become a target?

Everett told Castle only what he needed to know. But now, Castle had the notebook and had to do something with it. He had to protect it until someone who knew what it meant appeared.

Castle wanted to run. Running was also natural to him. It was a trait, a straight-line behavior inherited from time and a thousand generations. He had to survive.

He hunkered over Everett, patted his pockets looking for a key, a tool, things he might need. He found keys—no use. Coins—no use.

He would need money.

He went to the closet.

He searched Everett's jacket.

He found a billfold.

A passport.

But the billfold was empty.

That puzzled Castle. Where was the money? And the cards? A dozen cards each with a different name, but not one with the name Everett.

The passport alone said Everett.

Who was Everett?

Coming around now, alert, Castle thought.

He centered on the name Biggs.

Biggs and his people—Randall, the short man, the tall man. Centrex people. People who would have seen to it that Everett, whatever his name was, had the necessary papers in any name that he needed.

The name was important. That was why Everett didn't want to be seen. He didn't care about the name. He'd sign it anywhere. Only a few people knew he was using it, and they were his people.

Biggs. He was Centrex. He could be contacted. Castle didn't know names, didn't know codes. If Everett wasn't a name, Biggs might not be either.

Castle returned to the body. Patted the back and the thick middle. There, he found what he was missing. The thickening around the belly wasn't flab, but a money belt that contained hundred-dollar bills.

The thieves. Were they thieves? They'd have taken more than the briefcase. But Castle had interrupted them.

His hands were thick with blood. His own? Everett's? The fleeing man?

Leaving Everett, Castle returned to his room. He cleaned away the remnants of violence. He then dressed. He then sat on the bed with the notebook in hand.

He studied it. Should he cut it open and read it?

What good would that do?

He didn't need to know what was in the notebook. Not now.

He would hand it over to Cathay just as it was.

And then, Castle rose.

The longer he stayed in the hotel, the greater the danger. He had to find Cathay. He glanced at his watch.

The world had changed in a short time.

He folded the paper and tucked it into his pocket along with the cards, the money, and the passport.

When they found Everett, he would be nothing but a dead giant. No name. It would take time to identify him.

Castle wrapped the notebook and the knife up in the front page of La Voz and he exited into the corridor. He had to disappear until morning. The night would hold him until he found Cathay.

Cathay was the link he had. Everything depended on Cathay.

*****

Castle worked his way out of the Hotel Cordoba and burrowed into the darkness. It settled around him as he slid without purpose or direction. It was born in him, the instinct particular to small things. To survive meant to use the thickness of the dark as cover.

He inched into the street, slithering from doorway to doorway, those small dark islands.

38

Rounding a corner, he stopped. Just ahead, in a shaft of light coming from a night club, he saw a pair of feet. An open taxi door. Legs emerged. The woman they supported was tall. Unsteady, she stumbled, turned. Castle saw her face. He fused into the shadows as a man followed the woman from the car. A second women emerged. The trio went into the night club. The tall woman was Inga the flight attendant. The man was Federico Talavera, the poet. The second woman was Genobeba.

The taxi pulled away.

Castle crouched when he heard the rattle of a jeep. The vehicle turned the corner, paused in front of the night club then pulled down a few doors and parked.

The white helmets of four Nacionales— glistening insect shells in the dim light. Castle had to decide—run or stay. He gritted his teeth, about to step out of the doorway.

The Nacionales in the jeep smoked and joked. The driver kept glancing back at the doorway to the night club.

—They'll be here soon, — one of them said.

—Always late, Rodriguez, probably screwing his mother-in-law. —

The other three laughed.

—You should be a poet, Nando, then you could fuck blond gringas instead of making straw till your hand hurts. —

—That son of a bitch won't fuck anybody after tonight, — Nando replied.

Castle's chest tightened. He clutched the newspaper with the notebook and the knife. Leave them in the doorway? He knew what the Nacionales were going to do. He couldn't stop it. He couldn't move. If he walked into the street, they might search him. If he stayed where he was, he might be safe as they were watching the night club. Waiting.

Castle thought of the women—Inga, Genobeba—knowing the Nacionales would take them because they were with the poet. What would they do? Who was Rodriguez?

He gathered up his fear. Closed his eyes. Held the package against him. Felt the chill.

He opened his eyes when a second jeep with Nacionales arrived. They were followed by a third and a fourth.

They blocked off the street. Their boots clattered on the street.

At a signal from the commander—Rodriguez? —the strike force attacked the door to the night club and the street erupted as the Nacionales swarmed into the club, firing in the air, kicking, shouting and from inside came a burst of music—a huayno—then screams and gunfire. The Nacionales burst out of the club and ahead of them were the three-Inga, the Poet, Genobeba—hands bound, shoved hard, the women stumbled, the poet was bleeding from his face and in the light of the club,

Castle saw the face of the commander and he was smiling as he clubbed the poet to his knees. He said,

—Fucking commie degenerate. —

Castle oozed into the night and slid along the side of the building to the corner expecting to feel a hand on his shoulder, to hear bullets. Expecting to die.

Behind him, the sound of gunfire continued. He did not look back.

TEN

Fear is a chemical froth that bubbles up with the event that produces it. Fear lives buried in the body, an evolved composite of archaic survival devices riding on genes that cause it to react before the mind sees what the senses perceive. Danger. In times of danger, to think is to die.

Under attack, mammals show their reptilian past and regardless of brain capacity, function as conduits for their atavistic chemical reactions. In the past, before the blade, before the bomb, survival depended on flight or fight, so the organism has access to both—pulse rate increases, bronchial tubes dilate, muscles expand with rich oxygenated blood and adrenaline and the body no longer notices its place in time or space so enters its chemical eternity. This response is the same on paved city streets of the moment or the ancient savannah of a million years ago and will persist even when cities no longer are.

Castle had passed through fear, had fallen into despair, and now wanted only to keep his eyes open long enough to finish what he had set out to do. His heart beat not with the pounding pulse of an attack, but with the tense drumming of a man running—his skin hot, his sweat held the peculiar odor of epinephrine exuding through his pores. He knew this—

They had found Everett.

They had identified Castle as the killer.

Killer. The word was strange. Running, he had saved his own life, but now, something he hadn't counted on—being named the killer. La Voz said that the consulate had no record of anyone named Castle. His identity was a mystery.

A Colonel Rodriguez, of the Policia Nacional, said that the killer was in Ayahuantu illegally, said that the borders were sealed, said that the killer would be seized.

Castle pored over the descriptions witnesses had given of him and he smiled seeing that they were each so different that it wasn't certain if the killer, Castle, was one man or three. Three men or six. That ambiguity released his camouflage. He could not travel as a foreigner. He had to become an Indian.

Until he found Cathay, Castle had to change his approach because he was no longer rushing toward an objective, but he was fleeing his pursuers as well. He knew that if the Nacionales took him, he would never see Cathay or anyone again.

*****

The address Everett had written was in Miraflores. The streets there were wide, the houses inhabited by well-to-do people who hid behind high fences topped with shards of broken glass. There was no garbage on the paved streets, no beggars hobbling on crutches.

Miraflores' main connection to Huañuscacuchu was the one thing that prevented Castle from approaching Cathay's house—the regular patrol of the Nacionales in their Jeeps. There was no reason for an Indian to see Cathay.

As the patrol made its pass, Castle saw a young woman come out of the house. She carried a large woven basket. She wore the blue dress and the white apron of a servant. A woman. A woman Castle could talk to. A patrol of Nacionales he could not.

She walked past the Nacionales ignoring their propositions, their comments, their vulgarities. She turned the corner onto the boulevard, stopped at the bus stop. Castle approached her, asked if she was going to the market and he changed his shape, his color, the tint of his skin and she smiled at him.

By the time they reached Quespiyiri Terminal, they had passed a dozen patrols of Nacionales and Castle had found out that Don Ricardo, as she called Cathay in her subservient dialect, was not in Huañuscacuchu, but had gone to the mountains for the Festival of Santiago de Pachakuyuy. He had left the evening before with Señor Jacobs.

—How long will he be gone? —

—I don't know but I have to do the shopping because when he comes back, he will bring many gringos with him. —

—Where does he stay in Pachakuyuy? —

—Where he always stays. At Juntuuma, at the spa. —

—Have you been there? —

—No. Don Ricardo never takes servants with him. —

*****

Quespiyiri was a market center in Huañuscacuchu that was a hub for trucks and produce, for live animals, for men looking for work. Everything was in motion and the frenzy was counterpointed with smells—the scent of rotting vegetables, the aroma of baking bread, air thick with diesel fumes and the occasional scent of animal waste from the pigs, the llamas, and sheep.

Castle walked with Octavia as she filled her basket and he watched for Nacionales, but the activity, the coming and going seemed to keep them at their distance.

The market was also the main terminal for goods funneled through Huañuscacuchu to the provincial villages. Cathay was in Pachakuyuy. Castle had to go there.

Leaving Octavia to get on a bus for her return to Miraflores, Castle found a truck loading for a run. He convinced the trucker to let him help in return for passage to the mountains because he wanted to go to the festival.

It was late when Castle climbed into the back of the truck as it pulled out of Huañuscacuchu and ran into a downpour.

*****

Using the package with the notebook and knife as a headrest, Castle settled in. The rutted road, nothing more than a fragile scar cut into the cordillera, made it impossible to sleep. The rain turned the road to mud. The truck lurched over the ruts. Bottles of beer in their wooden crates rattled with the rhythm and sway.

Twice, the driver stopped to call Castle to help him clear the road of rockslides. And then, a checkpoint by Nacionales.

Castle came up sharp when they tossed the canvas cover aside and jumped into the back. The Nacionales, four of them, ignored him because it was a beer truck.

—Where are you going? —one of them asked the driver.

—Pachakuyuy, —the driver answered.

—Thirsty people in Pachakuyuy. —

—It's the nature of the saint, —the driver said, —a heavy sword creates a dry mouth. —

—Is your beer any good? —

—The best in Ayahuantu. —

—Then the saint won't miss a bottle or two. —

—We all have to sacrifice to the saint, — the driver said.

Beer in hand, the Nacionales waved the truck on.

Deeper into the mountains, the road became rougher. Castle fell asleep.

*****

At dawn, the driver jerked the truck to a stop and called Castle out.

Pachakuyuy, the enormous mountain that gave the town its name appeared as a cortège of thunder clouds peeled free for the early sun.

Castle was not as impressed as he might have been after a good night's sleep, but the mountain, a perfect volcanic cone, demanded he look at it.

The town was made of adobe. A constant brown broken by patches of white plaster. Along the main street, roofs had collapsed and the adobe turned back into mud.

Pachakuyuy was one of the vanishing groups of mountain cities that was entirely Indian. In its isolation, it had grown up semi-independent of the rest of the country and Spanish was a foreign language to most of its inhabitants. When they spoke the language of the conquerors, it was only to officials from the capital.

As with all the mountain towns, the streets were cobblestone, narrow, and not meant for the giant trucks that wormed their way along like wheeled larvae.

A truck blocked the street, forcing the early risers to press against the sides of buildings to pass. The walls were blank, windowless, rising high. The style was tempered by a touch of Spain, but the city was a relic of another time, its plan a copy of other minds.

The morning air was thick with the odor of burning dung, the fuel of the highlands where no trees grew, and now that pungency was tainted with diesel fumes as the remains of animals mixed through time, each powering some human enterprise. The Indians, as they watched the truck pass, covered their faces with scarves as if the air had become poison, as if the town, once safe in its isolation, was being lifted into a discomforting and disastrous present.

Santiago was a major saint.

His festival was the year's major event.

The festival was an open fete.

People from the smaller villages streamed into Pachakuyuy.

Held in the rainy season, and its distance from Huañuscacuchu kept the tourists away.

Vendors had set up stalls on the square turning it into a mosaic of canopies.

Spread out on red and blue blankets were the Indian goods—

Skirts, shawls, pullus.

Hunters from the selva carried monkeys, coati-mundis, and parrots that they offered either as food or as pets.

In this growing mash of bodies, Castle paid his debt by unloading the beer truck. No longer quick or cautious, he faded into the work, silent.

The main thing on his mind was knowing that he was now closer to Cathay. He had only to go to Juntuuma and it would be done.

With the truck empty, Castle refused the invitation of the trucker to make a run back to Huañuscacuchu. He said,

—I need sleep. —

—Sleep in the truck. —

—With you driving like a burro, no sleep. —

—Catch it next year, —the trucker said, —the saint'll still be here. —

—I won't be here next year. —

—Hey, the Fiesta of San Isidro is next week in Chacanahuayco. I can use you. You work hard. —

—No, the Nacionales are after me. —

—Nacionales? Fuck. All they want is beer and women. —

—How do I get to Juntuuma? —

—Juntuuma? Nothing there but a church and a spa. —

*****

Juntuuma was an hour walk from Pachakuyuy. Tired, Castle had to force his body to move. He had to see Cathay.

A kilometer from the market, Castle came to a boy who stood pounding a drum. Behind him were two groups. One was costumed and masked dancers the other in ancient military gear—helmets, shields, swords. The dancers' movement synched to the metallic plucking of a shoulder harp, the whine of quenas, and the yowl of the charango. They were Moros y Cristianos. Castle had seen them in many fiestas, always the same. The quenas reminded him of the blind quena player in the square in the city.

At every festival, groups like this one enacted the expulsion of the Moors from Spain. An act bathed in the blood of a history they had never read. It was a ritual dance commemorating the battles of the Spanish god against the Indian deities, battles in which the Sun always died.

As they passed, Castle moved aside. They were followed by other bands, Indians in mantas, llicllas, huipiles, and chukus dancing huaynos, handkerchiefs waving in rhythm to the music of the musicians playing sikus, panpipes, and conch shells.

Through all of this, paying little attention to it except for the cover it provided him, Castle squirmed until he saw men in military uniforms approaching the marchers. On the alert, his breath quick, eyes sharp, Castle felt behind his back the package of notebook and knife. He was worried.

They had gotten to the market fast.

Perhaps they had been there all along.

Perhaps they didn't know about him.

He had made it to Pachakuyuy without being discovered.

But now he was close enough to worry about mistakes.

But he had passed with the trucker. He could pass.

He was searching for an escape route when he realized that the men before him were not Nacionales. They were not wearing the white helmet. Their uniforms were of a different color and cut. They didn't carry machineguns. He didn't understand.

He felt like an insect trapped in a glass cage, his shell bumping against the wall. And then he felt himself being pushed along the adobe wall of the building just as the clouds holding back let loose a torrent catching Castle and the dancers and the musicians and the men in military uniforms.

And the crowd crushed Castle inside a church.

He stepped into the doorway and saw them—the uniforms.

Eyes fixed on the spot where he stood, they rushed at him.

Castle felt for the package at the small of his back. Trapped.

The church was cold. The rain brought a chill, a chill lightened by the flames of hundreds of altar-candles. Covered with sweat, Castle knew he had lost. It had been too easy.

He lost his sense of purpose.

He wanted to hide.

His instincts said find a dark place and crawl into it.

Wait for danger to pass.

If they caught him, they got the package. He couldn't let them have the package.

Fatigue. Anxiety. No thought.

The package. He had to put it somewhere. Hide it.

Without the package he would be nothing.

His eyes flickered with the flickering candles and he slithered through the press of bodies and the odors and the sounds until he stood under Santiago, the gilded figure glistening like a god of war in golden armor high on the altar in a place of honor under the rood and surrounded by a halo of tapers.

Santiago, the demi-god of the conquerors.

It was to him that they begged for strength in their wartime. It was he who made their sword arms strong.

Santiago.

The men in uniform were inside the portal. Castle watched them scout, their eyes not on the golden saint or the alter, but on the faces and each sweep of their eyes seemed to make him swell up, huge and awful, but he knew he melted into the mass of brown faces and small bodies.

He turned to the altar where he saw the priest.

A small stocky man. Without glasses, he was very much like Castle. Setting his back to the wall, Castle scooted down the wall past the alter although his brain said hide, his body said flee.

The priest negotiated with a group of Indian women who begged him to say a special mass for them.

—Why do you need a special mass? —He said.

—-For the dying and the dead, —a woman replied.

—How many? —the priest said.

—Many, many, they are dying with the plague. —

—The plague? In Pachakuyuy? —

Castle oozed past the alter until he came to a door.

Inside, a chair, a table, a small bed.

On the table, an ashtray with a still smoldering cigarette.

A large armoire held a habit, a coat, an overcoat.

A grey suit hung over a pair of muddy boots.

The armoire was ripe with the smell of mold.

Castle took the package with the notebook and knife, and, standing on the chair, placed the package on top of the armoire. He replaced the chair, grabbed the habit and hat. Pulling his poncho off, he tugged the habit over his head, put on the hat. Everything fit him.

He re-entered the church where the priest was still talking to the women. The women, on their knees, feet protruding from beneath their skirts, listened to his Latin. Everything he said was magic.

Castle watched the uniforms sifting through the nave, their eyes searching the crowd and then he pushed open the side door and dipped out into the rain.

ELEVEN

The mozo led Castle to Don Ricardo's room and left him standing in the corridor. He said nothing about Castle's habit. There were many orders of priests in Ayahuantu.

Castle took a cleansing breath. Fatigued. Sweaty. But he was satisfied. He had made it.

He knocked.

Cathay opened. He was polite but cold. He looked through Castle with the impatience of a man who dismissed religion and charlatans who practice it for their private political ends. He spoke in Spanish.

—What do you want, padre? —

Castle measured the man, let the words splash over him. He should have felt relief to be there, but from somewhere in his weary brain, a warning arose.

Cathay had the polished look peculiar to men who lead corporations. There was a not-quite concealed brutality etched in his face. He would be at home in pinstripes, Bermuda shorts on a beach in the Caribbean, or wearing a bush jacket and holding a large bore rifle as he stood over an elephant with five-foot tusks.

He carried himself with the ease of a man used to power. He belonged where money was made. Smooth. Graying hair at the temples. Steel-blue eyes, square chin, manicured nails. He added up to persuasion, self-assurance, success, and arrogance.

Castle's first reaction was to let his doubt fade. This was a man Everett would know and trust. This was the right thing. This was why he had come. He said,

"Mr. Cathay, you don't know me, but I have to talk to you."

Cathay hesitated. He glanced up and down the hallway. He said,

"If it's a donation you're after, can it wait? I'm expecting a visitor."

"Can't wait," Castle said.

He darted past the man in the doorway and into the room. It smelled of cologne. A strong cologne. Seated in two chairs at a large desk, there were two people—a man and a woman. Cathay said,

"What is this?"

"I'm not a priest."

"You've gotten yourself up in a disguise for the fiesta then? I don't know how they'll take having you made up as a priest around here."

"My name is Castle."

"Castle? What do you want?"

"I was with Everett."

The man and the woman at the desk, speaking at once, said,

"Everett? Mr. Cathay."

"I don't know any Everett," Cathay said.

His composure bled away into a wary stance, alert. Eyes sparkling. Castle expected caution. A pseudo-priest wearing muddy *ushutas*, a hat set on top of his head like a dinner plate. More than caution, Castle expected a gun in the hand. Castle said,

"He's dead."

"Dead?" The man and the woman stood. Cathay held out a hand.

"The notebook," Castle said. "He told me to bring you the notebook."

"Give me a moment, Castle."

Cathay turned to the man and woman and he said, in Chinese,

—Please, forgive this intrusion Mr. Huai, Miss Lin. I don't know this man but he says he is with Everett. Will you please leave us? I'll come to you when I have this sorted out."

—Of course, — Mr. Huai said. —Miss Lin? —

—Yes, yes. Later.—

They shook hands with Cathay and left the suite. Cathay faced Castle. He said,

"Everett told you? The notebook?"

"I'm beat, Mr. Cathay. I need to get some rest. But yes. The notebook. For you."

"Ah. The notebook. I'm sorry. I didn't understand. I didn't expect you to deliver it."

He glanced at the door. Castle felt a chill. It wasn't right. He wanted this to be the end. He knew something was wrong. He said,

"Who are you friends?"

"Mr. Huai," Cathay said, "Miss Lin."

"Chinese?"

"Yes, Chinese. But I don't understand."

"It was in the papers. They think I did it."

"Did what?" Cathay said.

"Murdered him. Look. I've been on the move. Got to get out of Ayahuantu."

"How did you locate me?"

"Talked to your people in the city."

"No one knows I'm here."

"Who were you expecting?"

"What?"

"Expecting. You said a visitor."

"Not you."

"You knew he was dead," Castle said.

Cathay leaned on the back of an armchair. He said,

"Did you read this..uh...notebook Everett gave you?"

"No. Could have. Didn't."

Cathay's smile melted into genuine puzzlement.

"Dedication. Of course. Since you were with Everett, you know what this is all about."

"Didn't tell me anything," Castle said. "Never told me anything about anything."

"I see. Did you talk to Jacobs?"

"Jacobs? Don't know Jacobs. Need sleep, Cathay. Three nights, no sleep."

"Yes, yes. You didn't talk to Jacobs."

"Didn't talk to anyone until I talked to you. Chinese?"

"Yes, yes, Chinese. Amazing. I think the best thing would be for you to let me have the book and then you can get on with your business."

Cathay held out a hand in expectation. Castle looked at him. Book? There was no book. Cathay didn't know about the notebook. Castle couldn't get on with his business because being there was his business. He had come to Pachakuyuy to hand over the notebook. Not a book.

Castle felt the canine in him holding onto a bone. Hanging on to what he had was a command built into every cell in his body—hang on to what he had. He couldn't let go. The bone was everything he had. He said,

"Don't have it."

It felt good. Hearing words come from a deep place, a strange place as if coming from someone else. Cathay sniffled. He said,

"Look here, Castle. What are you trying to pull?"

"No. Not pulling anything."

Castle felt his brain struggling to undo the words, to find out what they meant, but he couldn't. The words were like large wooden blocks that he shoved but they didn't move. What language was he speaking? Quechua? Aymara? English? Chinese? Sleep, he needed sleep. Cathay said,

"You want money?"

—Money? No. Sleep. Sleep. —

"What?"

"Sleep," Castle said.

"You come in here, you can't produce this book you've killed a man for…"

—Didn't kill, — Castle shouted. English. English. "Don't have it on me."

"Cathay! Jacobs."

The knock on the door brought Cathay to point. The tension in his face made him ugly, a mask twisted into knots.

Castle watched, his eyes going in and out of focus. Where was he? Why was he? Who was he? Cathay glowered at him then went to the door.

"Jacobs," Cathay said, "you're late."

"I saw the Chinese. Are they in? Just blew in from Huañuscacuchu. Those dumb bastards have fucked up everything."

"This is Castle," Cathay said.

He held up his hand. Jacobs rolled to a stop.

Castle blinked. He felt tension in his stomach. He wanted to vomit. The man had a name. It was Jacobs. Shorty. Shorty was Jacobs.

Castle knew him. But instead of a three-piece suit, he wore khaki, military khaki. He wore boots. He wore a field cap. A pistol strapped to his side. Jacobs looked first at Cathay then at Castle and then his hand strayed to the pistol in the holster. He barked,

"How in hell…"

"Take him to Quillomayu Jacobs. The authorities think Mr. Castle had a hand in Everett's murder."

"He's not a priest," Jacobs said. "He is one of Everett's idiots."

"No, he's not a priest. I don't want the authorities to find him. You can understand my reasoning in that."

"Quillomayu?"

"You'll take care of him, won't you?"

"Okay," Jacobs said.

Castle watched the two men. He felt like a piece of property. He didn't want Jacobs to take care of him. He didn't like Jacobs now and for the same reason he hadn't liked him the first time they met in New York—Shorty was a rotten little bastard whose greatest joy was kicking the crap out of other small men.

"Take him straight out there," Cathay said. "I'll be out later. Couple of things I have to square away. What?"

"You'll come out?"

"You send a jeep for me."

Jacobs was silent. He looked at Castle. He shrugged. He said,

"You know what you're doing, Cathay. Come on Father Castle."

Castle's head was buzzing, his ears ringing. Nothing made any sense. And then he remembered the habit. He followed Shorty out to a jeep where two men, wearing the same khaki and brown uniform Jacobs had on, saluted and Castle recalled where he had seen it before but his muddled brain couldn't sort it out. Too much information. Too many questions. Like a kid at the zoo, all he saw was the duck. Uniforms. The church. They were part of Jacob's security apparatus. Jacobs was head of security for Centrex. He was in the field. He would wear a uniform. That made sense.

Climbing into the back seat of the jeep, Castle plopped down with a hard thud. Shorty climbed into the front, crisp as a general running a convoy. Castle hated that crispness. Shorty had had sleep so he could be crisp. His energy. Castle resented that too. With sleep, he'd have energy too.

"Crisp," Castle said. "Crisp, very crisp."

Jacobs turned in his seat. He snarled as his eyes raking Castle were flashing knives. He said,

"You shithead."

"Sleep," Castle said.

In his mindlessness he wondered why Cathay hadn't taken the notebook why he hadn't said a word about the notebook and that was why Castle had come—to deliver the notebook and now it didn't make sense and Castle knew that the part of his brain that was working would have continued to work even had he been a reptile or a lobotomized primate or a marsupial but it was part that never slept, and he needed sleep, and he was going to sleep...Sometime...

"Look, asshole," Jacobs said.

Castle looked at the face scowling at him, but it wasn't human. It was like a Halloween mask, a kid dressed up like a soldier. Castle smiled. He felt his eyes droop. He said,

"Trick or treat."

He wanted to sleep, but it wasn't going to happen. That was how it happened sometimes—when you ought to sleep your brain won't let you and without sleep you go crazy and Castle knew he was at the limit.

Jacobs' finger jabbed Castle in the forehead. Castle smiled. Halloween. Jacobs said,

"You fucker. You caused me more god-damned grief but this is going to be the last time…"

Castle shook his head, his eyes fluttered. He said,

—Fuck you, you llama turd. —

TWELVE

From Juntuuma, the jeep veered off the road heading away from Pachakuyuy. The jerkiness of the ride kept Castle awake. They came to a barrier guarded by two uniformed, armed men who raised the barrier—a steel pole with a sign saying Danger on a plaque.

They entered a large barbed-wire ringed compound. A dozen adobe buildings plastered white. Guard towers. Armed men. Sentries. Light military vehicles—half-tracks, jeeps, trucks—in rows. All painted the same somber shade of brown. No markings. No signs.

Castle sat forward, grasping the back of the seat. He said,

"What is this, Jacobs?"

"It's a military camp, numbnuts."

Shorty barked an order as the jeep ground to a stop. A detail of security men, all in brown, grabbed Castle and hauled him out of the jeep. He stumbled, crashing through a door that sprang back. He fell to a knee, stood, confused.

He turned into Shorty's hand in which there was a pistol that landed with a sharp thunk against Castle's head.

Castle staggered. Jacobs said,

"Sleeping potion, padre."

Jacobs then kicked Castle in the face.

*****

He didn't want to wake up, but the pain was kicking him hard. His jaw was on fire. When he opened them, his eyes felt like jellyfish tossed into a burning sun. His tongue probed the inside of a bloody mouth. He was surprised to find that it was his own and his tongue snaked through a hole where his teeth should have been. When he took a breath, his breath hung up in his chest behind a wall of hurt. *Jacobs. The despicable little bastard.*

He coerced his burning eyes to focus. They fixed on a wall. Then, a wooden floor. Brain. Brain, are you working? No, came the reply. He wiggled as he mapped out the space—he was on his belly, his hands tied in front of him. The ache in his gut was from his hands pressed into his diaphragm. He hunched forehead toward his toes and the pain slid from his diaphragm to his testicles.

He looked for his feet. He couldn't see them. No feet. *Jacobs has cut off my feet.*

Grunting, he took a shallow pain-laced breath and twisted until he saw two pairs of boots. Very black boots. Muddy soles. Pants. Pants tucked into the tops of the boots. Men wearing pants and boots. Muddy boots. Rain.

He opened his mouth. His jaw was mushy, formless, a flesh amoeba. He needed to touch his lips. His jaw. Nothing could hurt that much unless it was broken. He groaned and grunted and looked at his guards.

They stared at him the way fishermen watch an abomination they have snared in their nets. Castle said,

—Gentlemen. —

He inched his way onto his knees. He was on his way to upright when one of the pairs of boots walked across the room and pushed him back down. Castle said,

—You're not gentlemen. —

—Go tell the short one that this pig scrotum has come back from the dead, — Boots said to his companion.

Castle's language gear shifted into low as he listened to the words. *Argentinos. Don't let me be in Argentina.* The cloud-pain dropped onto his head. *Let me be in hell. Let me be in Dade County or even Fresno, but not Argentina.*

The Boot poked under his chin. Pain down his neck. He said,

—That hurts. —

He rolled over and once more stared at a wall.

He changed position so that in his worm's eye view of the world, he had one friend—the wall. He saw a tripod. Metallic. Black. Deadly looking. The tripod was connected to a very real fifty caliber machinegun. *Argentina.*

Castle was certain of three things:

Everett had been playing with some heavy-duty people.

His efforts to locate Cathay had backfired.

He was as good as dead.

In the part of his brain that was working, there was a touch of a question—what the hell is going on?

Voices.

He heard them arguing. The door opened. Castle didn't raise his head. He knew who it would be when boot heels snapped together with a familiar click.

"He came into my room babbling about a book Everett had given him. Your people didn't miss anything else, did they, Jake? I hope to hell not because it would just make me think you can't pull this thing off."

"He didn't have anything on him," Jacobs said. "And it was a stupid fucking idea to bring this piece of shit out here, Cathay."

Castle squirmed. It wasn't good that they had reduced him to a piece of shit. It couldn't end well. Nothing good ever came from being a piece of shit. Cathay said, in the tone of voice a CEO would use on his board of directors,

"He's awake."

He sat on a box of ammunition that had US Army written on it.

"You're too sensitive," Cathay said. "What other course was there? Keep him in my room like a pet snake? This man says he has some kind of a book. Well, what the hell kind of book is it?"

"This is the first I've heard about any fucking book," Jacobs said.

"And that's a failure, Jake. You knew Everett. You had access to the files."

"I didn't blow it, Cathay. It was those clowns in Huañuscacuchu."

"If Everett weren't dead, I'd begin to wonder about a double-cross."

"Well, if it's a trap, he fell into it," Jacobs said.

"The question now," Cathay said, "is what did Everett tell our friend here."

"What difference does it make?"

"The difference is that they know something we don't."

"You couldn't get the time of day out of Everett. Look at that stupid broad. She didn't know shit. This guy knows something, I guarantee it."

"She didn't say anything about a book, did she, Jake?"

"There was no fucking book in that office."

"So we don't have any idea what she knew because you and your thugs...That's one reason I never liked this idea of you splitting your time. You see? Now, if you'd been here when they questioned her, that woman might have told us something. But. As it stands, the little padre here knows about a book that we've never heard of, Jake. That could be a problem because you know what a fanatic Everett was."

"I got you the tapes," Jacobs said.

"And what do they tell us? They don't tell us who he saw the last two times he was here. If you'd handled things...Frankly, the Argentine is too brutal..."

"He gets results."

"All he got was a dead woman," Cathay said. "And all we need is a bunch of Nacionales poking around up here."

"Vargas," Jacobs said. "I ought to gut that bastard."

"That would be one solution, wouldn't it?" Cathay said, "but I worry about our friends Castle and Everett."

"The man's dead," Jacobs said. "The bottom line is asshole here is ignorant."

"You're awfully certain for a man whose people almost botched this whole thing, Jake. All the information in that book could ruin us if it gets in the wrong hands and by wrong hands, I mean Vargas."

"You don't know there is any information."

"How close was Everett to a deal? Who was he dealing with? We don't know, Jake. What if some of our friends are playing both sides?"

Cathay rubbed his hands together, shrugged as if letting go and looked at Castle. Castle watched his face, watched it change shape from puzzled to violent, eyebrows arched, lips in a hard, straight line. Cathay turned back to Jacobs. He said,

"How did your people lose the tapes, Jake? The tapes were going to clarify some things, but what did we get? Nothing. How did your people lose them when they left Huañuscacuchu? In this country with fifty automobiles on the road at any time, you couldn't follow one car."

Castle rocked back and forth. The dead woman. Burying her. The suitcase. And then his mind jerked back to Villareal and Tarma and the woman, Marta, and her fixation on alien eggs and then out of a miasma Randall emerged lying on the bed in the hotel the day she picked him up at La Guardia and Castle smelled her, how good she smelled, would she smell that he had become a piece of shit...

"And how did they miss his visitor the night they killed him? Who was that, Jake?"

"I don't know. I don't know anything."

"You hired these men, Jake. You trained them. You brought them here. If this is the kind of job you're going to do when we've bought this rat hole, I don't think we could hold on for five minutes if Vargas quits playing along."

"Biggs and me, we tried to talk Everett out of this guy."

"What if Castle isn't what you say he is?"

"They dragged this little piece of shit out of a sewer someplace."

"The little pieces make the puzzle, Jake. It doesn't matter that you yourself didn't create the problem, but people want this project to work, so maybe they ask if you're..."

"Not big enough to get the job done?" Jacobs laughed.

Castle watched the little man's neck jiggle. Castle wanted to laugh along with him but he hurt too much. Jacobs said,

"I'll deliver. Wait till after the elections before you go jump off any bridges."

"You're right," Cathay said. "But it could be essential to know what's in that book and who Everett was talking to."

"You want this little shit to talk?" Jacobs said. "I'll make him talk."

Jacobs jerked Castle to his feet. Cathay slid off the ammo box and stood in a corner. Jacobs shook Castle, hard. He said,

"Okay father, you've got a book and I want it."

Jacobs smacked Castle in the ear. Stinging. Castle wobbled. He looked at Cathay who stood arms folded as he turned Shorty loose. He said,
"I don't want him dead until I have the book, Jake."

THIRTEEN

The jail was a mud and straw hut with four iron bars in a lone window. A single room. Wooden door. A wooden-frame bed made of cut strips of llama hide. A single chair—useless because it had four legs, one of them cracked. No toilet. No water.

Castle lay on the bed, the llama hide strips cutting into his back, staring at the ceiling of stakes covered with straw, and he remembered the bed in the hotel in Huañuscacuchu and the sweaty session with Randall and how she said nothing after but got dressed and left him.

It was getting dark.

Cathay had been gone a long time.

When Cathay came back without the notebook, Castle knew Jacobs would kill him.

He knew Jacobs would enjoy killing him.

Randall? Marta? Alien eggs?

He knew that he hated Jacobs.

The dead woman now buried in the altiplano? What? Castle did not want to kill Jacobs because Castle was a good man and he knew as he lay on the bed stretched out on the llama thongs that he was being used by bad men. He remembered kneeling beside her in the office in Huañuscacuchu and he remembered feeling her pulse, his eyes roving to the severed breast, the gash in her side that came from a heavy blade—a bayonet, a machete—feeling like he'd been hit in the gut with a boxing glove loaded with lead.

Jacobs.

His fingerprints were smeared all the way from New York to Juntuuma. What was going on? New York. Miami. Ayahuantu. Tarma. Pachakuyuy. Juntuuma. Everywhere he looked, Jacobs...

Castle rolled over and his jaw hurt. Every time his jaw zinged with pain, Castle's hatred for Jacobs grew stronger and he was glad he'd decided to lie about the notebook. Jacobs. Cocky. Bastard.

He had to get to Pachakuyuy.

He had to get the notebook.

But first he had to get out of the locked room.

And then, maybe he would kill Jacobs.

And Cathay.

Definitely Cathay.

Castle stood. He went to the door. Two guards were talking about the fiesta they were missing. They talked about fornication. They talked about beer. Castle knew they were Argentinos. The fact that they were Argentinos interested him and it was unsettling to know that Jacobs had an international mercenary force working in Ayahuantu. Why does Centrex need a security force in Ayahuantu? Private army. Mercenary force. Not security. Machiavelli didn't have good things to say about mercenaries because the mercenary's only loyalty is to money. Mercenaries meant money. Money meant rich men, rich corporations. Rich corporations spending their money on arms and the men. Returning to the window, Castle fingered the bars embedded in the adobe.

He yanked.

Pain shot up his neck into his jaw.

He twisted two of the bars but they didn't give.

He squatted to look at the chair. Pry bars. He had to loosen the llama strips to get the wooden legs free. Quiet. Any noise would give him, at most, a few seconds before the Argentinos broke in on him and broke his arms. Besides if he got out, he still had to get out of the compound wearing a priest's habit that made him more conspicuous than an erupting volcano. Still....

Castle grabbed the bars again. Pain raced through him. Jacobs.

Blinking back tears to kill the pain, he looked out the window. Mountains. Clouds. No sun now. It had been raining and the peaks were chewed up in gray clouds like fangs in flesh. It was an awesome, inspiring, touristy sight but Castle absorbed it without a twitter of aesthetic vibration in his body. Pain.

First—get out of jail.

Then—murder the Argentinos who had helped murder Allende's Chilenos.

Then—kill Jacobs who he didn't want to kill but it was written now, in the pain in his jaw, in his neck, in his back. He was pain and because he was pain, he was going to kill Jacobs.

But first he had to get out of jail before Cathay returned.

There was only one way out—through the window.

Back at the door, Castle checked the guards.

They were now standing ten meters away, still talking about women's breasts and fornication but still with some interest in drinking.

Castle, working as fast and quiet as he could, broke the legs loose from the chair seat—with each creak of the wood, he stopped.

Each twist of the llama thews sent Jacobean pain down his neck and up into his jaw. The wood was tough. It yielded in agony itself, and after three tries, Castle held two solid wooden legs and three long strips of llama hide.

He carried them back to the window.

He tied the thews around the two middle bars and using one chair leg twisted the thews into a knot and continued twisting but—nothing.

He doubled the thews and then inserted both chair legs and twisted while breathing through his mouth which caused him to whistle because Jacobs had kicked out his teeth. Through pain, whistling, breathing as he worked, he watched the bars bend.

He let go. Fifteen centimeters. A gap. A way out.

He listened for the guards.

He felt dizzy, hungry.

Was the floor dancing under him?

He steadied himself. The weakness, the dizziness—Jacobs had beaten in.

He stuck his arm through the gap, then his head, then his shoulder. It hurt.

He squeezed his chin and collapsed in a lighting strip of pain that ran up his back into the empty tooth sockets. His ears rang. He sagged. Fifteen centimeters. Not enough. Just not enough.

He hit it again. This time the bars moved closer together. They gave, small cracks grew in the adobe and a small chunk broke out and fell to the floor.

Progress.

He cinched the thews again and twisted just as he heard

—Carajo! —

Castle dropped the chair legs, the thews spun battering the adobe wall sending more chunks to the floor and Castle knew he was dead.

A guard peered through the half-open door.

Castle heard the guard fumbling with the lock on the chain on the door and he grabbed the chair legs now free from the thews and skipped to the door—pain all the way from his feet to his teeth—but he knew they would shoot him when they broke through the door but they were still fumbling with the lock and Castle realized that they didn't have a key.

Jacobs. He didn't trust anyone.

Castle laughed but staggered into the wall, dizziness again.

A few seconds more and he'd have been out. How far? Where would he go?

Dizzy again. The floor was dancing, and then he realized that he wasn't dizzy and it wasn't just the floor quivering but the whole building trembled and the guards were still shouting but not at him and Castle glanced out the window to watch the mountains shaking like the tassels on a midnight stripper and the jail galloped up and down and outside more voices joined the shouting and there was the wound of engines starting.

The door cracked open. Castle wheeled. The guard had smashed the lock with his rifle and skidded into the room but his first step was short and the roof of the jail collapsing battered him and he went down and timbers slammed Castle, a new pain tearing at his arm and the roofbeams crushed the bed in a hail of muck and rock and straw.

Castle knew he had been shot.

The guard looked at him.

The earth jumped again and another wave rolled and snapped the ground like a whip cracking.

Castle and the guard stared at one another. Castle felt the vibrating as if men were using jackhammers. Castle took a step toward the guard. The guard, on his feet, shouted and turned and ran.

The wall of the jail lurched. Castle sprang to the pile of debris in the middle of the room and turning, he saw the wall, popping and cracking, split in two.

Castle headed for the door.

Then, like two dominoes falling, the walls of the jail crashed and Castle stood, one wall in front of him, the other behind him and he felt the rush of air and then there was quiet.

He stepped between fallen walls and walked out into the early evening through a rush of bodies and no one paid him any attention and so he ran.

He ran and he kept on running.

*****

The earthquake destroyed the Feast of Santiago. Pachakuyuy, in the shadow of the mountain whose name was synonymous with earthquake, had been destroyed before. The ground cracked—teeth of gigantic dogs crushing bones—and earth rolled in waves. The people were not afraid of the earthquake but they knew the worst had not yet come.

In the silence after the shock wave, the town quivered, walls collapsed, cracks broke the streets and in the silence, people turned to the mountain that hung above the town but they did not run until they heard the rumbling. Earth-thunder. Unlike thunder with its light, this was a dark sound, sound that didn't fade but with time grew louder.

The huayco.

Broken free from the mountain, waves of rock and mud rolled down murdering everything fixed or moving.

Castle approached Pachakuyuy. He met a wave of refugees. He pressed on to the town until he saw the wall of the huayco—a liquid brown undulating serpent.

He threaded through a flowing crowd of children, women, masked revelers, herders trying to control their frightened animals, men, helpless to fend off the moving creature, all knowing that no man controlled the huayco, no man ever knew if it would turn, where it would turn, but they all knew not to hide because it did not forgive the hidden.

The huayco split the town in half as if a hand had drawn a line through the plaza, marking a channel for the mud to flow. The screech of boulders pulverized.

Castle came to the mouth of the beast and instead of running, he stopped to witness the confusion, to measure the devastation. He saw the fury of the huayco fading.

And again the town became silent. People who had been running, stopped at the same moment the huayco—a huge and weary earth-god—stopped flowing.

The end was sudden, the silence jarring. Then, out of the consuming darkness that lends its primordial touch of fear to chaos, came the first wailings of death.

The church, mother of miracles, jutted above the earth, outlined against the black and heavy sky, unscathed.

In the darkness, there was anonymity. Everyone alive fixed on the church, drawn towards its light.

Castle trudged through the muck, tripping over objects he knew were too soft to be stone. He was not bent on salvation of the spirit or comfort for the flesh. He wanted the notebook.

Castle entered. The hundreds of candles burning gave the nave a sinister glow. In the deep night, still smelling of mud and the peculiar sharp and flinty odor of crushed rock, the candles smeared the darkness with the only light. He hesitated. It would not have surprised him to find Cathay. Instead, he felt eager hands clutch at him.

—Padre, padre.—

Aged hands, covered with mud, blood? Grabbed at him.

—Padre, padre. —

Castle, not understanding why he attracted those hands, then remembered the robe.

He still wore the robe. It had taken a beating. Covered with mud. Torn. Caked with his blood, but in the chaos around him, it was a churchman's garment and he was wearing it. His swollen face, his broken teeth, showed that he had suffered.

Scanning for other priests, he saw black robes laboring in the glow of the church light—black robes worn by indispensable bodies. Castle was caught.

He glanced down the aisle to the door leading to the priests' room, and then at the broken women hunkered in corners, choking back tears, mouths quivering, eyes confused.

With a shrug, Castle stepped up to what was expected of him. He sent a boy for a doctor but the boy told him the doctor's house was gone.

—Send a runner to Juntuuma,— Castle said,—find doctors among the flat-landers. —

Castle set two men to build fires for boiling water. To a boy, he ordered to find what he could of food and medical supplies at the pharmacy.

—The owner is dead. — The boy said.

—Then bring what you find, — Castle said.

The huayco had taken out the road, he was told. It will be days before anyone from the capital can get in.

As casualties came to the church, Castle wound his way among the wounded, trying to dredge out of memory the words meant to mend broken souls but he found that in the misery, no one listened to what he said but when he mumbled and made the proper signs, his duty was fulfilled. Would other priests come from Juntuuma? Had the hotel there survived the quaking or had it been swallowed in its own ocean of mud? That was too much to hope for.

Cathay and his kind would survive. The rich men always survive.

*****

Early morning light filtered through the rose window of the church when Castle looked up to see men—figures of men—in the portal. Nacionales. A squad of them with their white helmets.

Castle glanced at the back of the church. The notebook. He could make a dash for freedom. Get the notebook. Read what it said. Get out of Ayahuantu.

The Nacionales wormed their way through the mass of bodies, stepping over the sleeping ones, avoiding the dead ones. Castle was prepped to make a break when the colonel leading the squad said,

—Padre, good morning. We are looking for a gringo. —

—Gringo, — Castle said. –He is a gringo. — He pointed at the Belgian priest who had come to the church at midnight. The colonel turned to the man. He said,

—Padre, we are looking for a criminal. A man who killed and robbed his companion in Huañuscacuchu. Can you help us? Have you seen this man? —

The gray-haired priest, hands on his hips glared at the colonel. With his thick Belgian accent, he said,

—Captain, you can see my problem. —

Castle turned his back, squatted, tucked a lliclla under the chin of a woman holding a baby. The woman smiled at Castle.

—I am a colonel, padre. —

—Colonel, captain, all are equal before God and both unimportant at this moment. —

—This is important, padre. —

—More important than helping these poor people? Look at them. Did you bring medical supplies with you? —

—No, padre. We have only ourselves. This man. —

—God doesn't care about the man you are seeking. Do you have supplies? —

—We were lucky to escape the huayco, padre. We walked ten kilometers because the road has vanished.—

—A radio then? You have a radio with which to call for doctors? —

—What can I say, padre? We came in search of this gringo. We did not expect such a catastrophe. —.

His habit sleeves were rolled up revealing stark white but muscular arms. His broad hands strong and tanned. The priest said,

—We need water, we need food. Save your soul and the souls of your men and help the ones who bleed. —

—This is an official mission, padre. I cannot have my men performing like nurses. —

—Of course, of course. What can be more important than one gringo while you plague me with your useless chatter, I have souls to tend. —

—This gringo is a criminal, padre. —

—I am a gringo, colonel. —

—Yes, but this man is a dangerous man. —

—And the earthquake? The huayco? They were not dangerous? They killed many compatriots, injured dozens of others. Where will my people sleep if they have no homes? What will they eat if they have no food? What do I care about one gringo? Bring me doctors. Bring me medicine and blankets. —

Castle looked up at the last words of the priest's harangue and what he saw made him wish for shadows. Jacobs. Jacobs and detail of his Argentine militia coming through the portal. They would not be so innocent as the colonel of the Nacionales. They knew what they were looking for.

Turning away from invaders, head bowed, shoulders slouched, Castle once again showed his chameleon skin by disappearing into the background and stepping into the priest's room.

The armoire. Still there.

The table.

The chair.

A priest lay on a cot, his arm in a sling.

He sat up, startled as Castle moved the chair to the armoire. The priest said,

—What are you doing? —

—Rest, padre, — Castle said. –Retrieving an amulet. —

From the top of the armoire, Castle felt the packet.

He grabbed it and as he leaped down, he slipped, hitting the floor, jamming his arm hard. In pain, he sat up, scurried, hands and knees, for the door.

He ran. He knew Jacobs' crew would come through the church and he had to be away.

The robe bound his feet. He stumbled. Hit his shoulder on the wall of the street. He held up at the corner. Shouts behind him.

The streets of Pachakuyuy were stone and adobe mazes. He did not have an internal map of the city.

No people there, only a grave silence that his footsteps, even in ushutas, broke as he charged across cobblestones—slipping, careening, sliding

The robe. He didn't have time to shed it. The robe was meant for godly work, for saving souls, for meditative strolls through colonnaded monastery arcades, not the furious dash of a hunted and broken man suffering from the pain of existence at the hands of evil through the streets of an earthquake ravaged Indian town.

He stumbled again. Lost his balance.

Came skidding around a corner where he found himself facing a battered Land Rover inching its way down the stone street.

Eyes fixed on the face of the old man behind the wheel, Castle braced himself, right arm, the hurt arm, outstretched for the crash against the windshield of the Rover that didn't come because the vehicle didn't have one.

He caromed over the hood of the Rover, landing on his bad arm in the seat beside the old man.

"Carajo. Puta madre. Chucha son of a bitch," the old man shouted. "I just killed me a padre, god man, huevon, carbon, porque'd you run out into the calle like a god damn mad hijo de puta for?"

Pain piercing him with blinding jabs, Castle almost laughed because the old man was speaking a pigeon of equal parts Spanish and English in the worst accent a human ear ever took in.

Castle grimaced, slid deeper between the seat and the firewall and he said, "Let's get the hell out of here, pappy."

"Jesus bald-headed Christ, a padre that hablas americano. And you ain't dead."

"No but I will be if you don't get me out of here. They're after me, pappy, and I'm hurting a whole bunch."

The old man looked at Castle. His gray felt hat was sweat stained around the band. His eyes, olive green beads nestled under faded eyebrows and sun-bleached lashes. His face looked as if it had etched to a depth of inches with powerful acid, then scoured with steel-wool and polished to a lustrous bronze by the wind. A bristly beard crept grayly over the bronze, a fungus-like growth that shone twice as bright against the bronze of his skin.

Head cocked, listening, Castle knew, to the same sounds of boots on cobblestone that he was hearing. Then, eyes squinted, he uncorked a stream of tobacco juice onto the wall of a house, slammed the Rover into reverse and backed down the street.

Castle breathed deep, moaning in his sanctuary.

The Rover bucked and leapt its way up a hill, spun a hard right at a speed that pinned Castle to the floorboard, and headed out of town—rocking over cobblestones—before shooting down a stone-fence-lined street. Outside the city, the Rover hammered the road until it turned away and bounded over a road free plain and Castle rose up and peered over the wind-shieldless dashboard. Behind the Rover, stood the mountain, its side scarred, laid bare as if it had been flayed by a powerful blade.

Castle gripped the packet in his good hand. Still there. The knife. The notebook.

Sighing and resting his head on the hard seat of the Rover, he knew one thing for sure. He had to get a new outfit.

FOURTEEN

The old man drew up on a quebrada kilometers from Pachakuyuy. From the lip of the quebrada, the floor of the valley stretched out blotted by the specter of the half-destroyed city sitting like a dirty brown swatch in a sea of fresh, dark mud.

Because the old man knew the mountains he had left Jacobs counting rocks somewhere along the way. The Nacionales chasing Castle had been outclassed by an old mountain man.

Despite his pain, when Castle turned to his savior to thank him, he laughed. The old man didn't have front teeth either. When he spoke it was in that mumbled mix of English cluttered with Spanish profanities and Indian words. Castle felt an instant affinity to him.

They were very much alike but the amity was tainted by a forty-five in a right hand, the pistol pointing at Castle like a big mouth snake.

The old man stood with one boot on the bumper of the Rover. He was not smiling. He said,

"Not often you get a padre up here in the cordillera that's had his face kicked in. But then, I reckon you ain't no padre."

Castle's face hurt all the way down to his shoulder. The arm that had caught the roofbeam of the collapsing jail was stiff. He grimaced. He said,

—Ari. —

"Ari? You talk runa simi?"

"Uh huh," Castle said, —Runa simi and castellano and Aymara."

"Well, runa simi or no runa simi I can see the hurt's on you bad, but I don't know nothin 'bout you 'cept you're runnin and you got hurt all over you and there's some bad hombres on your tail. 'Round here lately there's lots of reasons for a man to run hurt, so you're gonna tell me who from and why and who did that to you and I'd like you to make it quick."

The weapon aimed at his sternum didn't scare Castle, because he sensed that here was the one person he could tell the story to and live to tell it again. He sat on a rock, holding his arm to his side and started at the beginning. He mumbled as he learned to talk without teeth. His lisp didn't bother the old man who listened, nodding and wiping the back of his hand over his mouth after spitting. His eyes never left Castle's and the forty-five dipped away from dead center until the old man holstered it.

He grunted and nodded when Castle stopped talking and he fixed a one-eyed stare on Castle as he puckered his lips, cleared his throat and slid a plug of tobacco from his shirt pocket. He tore a piece from the plug. He said,

"You landed yourself in a viper's nest, son. You got this notebook on you?"

"And the knife they killed Everett with."

"That's pitiful, son. Here you come all that way lugging that thing and it almost got you killed. Ol' Jacobs plays for blood, he does."

"You know Jacobs?"

"I been in these hills for twenty years, yes I know Jake."

"You going to turn me over to him?"

"Nah. I figure you can get yourself in enough trouble. Don't look good for you though. What I hear, Jake goes after a man's head, he gets what he's going after."

"You been here twenty years. You've gotta know what they're doing."

"Jacobs and Cathay?"

"Yeah."

"At Quillomayu?"

"That's right."

"I know some of it, some of it I don't. You didn't tell me a whole lot that I don't already know, 'cept for the part about Everett."

The old man stopped. His manner changed. Castle sensed that there were secrets hidden in the old man and there was more to him than a forty-five and a Land Rover.

"Tell you—this other stuff, I been watchin it unwind for a couple years now. You don't see five gringos in a hundred years up here and all of a sudden you've got a god-damn army that stands out like warts on a baby's bottom."

"What do you think's going on?"

"Last year they was up at Chacanahuayco. That's where they put the big stuff-personnel carriers, tanks."

"Where's Chacanahuayco?"

"On the border. There didn't used to be much there but some wore out veins, but these fellas must have found something 'cause this past summer, they put up this campamento at Quillomayu and brought equipment and men in there."

"I think I've been in that campamento," Castle said. "Have you, Vic?"

"Quillomayu?"

"Yeah."

"You get anywhere close to it they chop the legs offa you."

"Doesn't make sense," Castle said. "Why does Centrex need an army?"

"Can't tell you, but a man's got no use for machineguns and bazooks unless he's up to no good. Now in this part of the world, up to no good can mean a lotta things. Like over in the Amazonas, I seen company armies. I mean regular outfits uniformed with guns, but they're company and they got no reason to be there except to kill Indians."

"Vic." Castle stood. The ground was swaying under him, lunging and spinning and he needed something to hang onto. Vic said,

"Take'er easy, son."

Castle looked at the old man but he couldn't focus. He took one step and fell on his face in the dirt.

*****

When he came to, Castle was on a strange bed wrapped in a layer of wool thick with smoke scent, sweat, and vague animal odors. He sat up. Expected to feel worse than he did. His hair was sweat-matted, his throat dry. He had a faint memory of a woman.

He was in a stone house, thatched ceiling. Open door.

In one corner, a fire burned under a large clay steaming pot. The pot was part of another cloudy recollection.

No furniture.

Dirt floor.

When he shoved the blanket away, he was stiff, but the pain was gone.

Testing his parts, he moved his head.

No neck pain.

Wiggled his jaw, light ache.

He opened his mouth. His teeth had not grown back.

Wiped at his face. No pain. The puffiness had vanished. His hand came away covered with a brown, gritty powder that he sniffed. Then tasted.

It wasn't mud but the taste brought back another memory, of touch, of someone holding him up, patting his face and he remembered thinking of butterfly wings on the wind, but then, that gentleness was tempered with a memory of foul tasting things shoved into his mouth.

He swung his legs to the dirt floor and heard a scurrying under his bare feet. Squealing, a herd of qoy—tiny and furry, brown and black— swarmed from under the bed and shot out the door. The pot. Guinea pigs.

Castle got to his feet. He stopped.

A small woman in the door.

She wore a stiff white hat, a lliclla over her shoulders, full skirt, no shoes. In her arms she clutched a bundle of fresh grass. She grinned at Castle. She said,

—Your fever is down now. —

Her eyes sparkled with a mystery. She squinted at him. The face was Indian, and the depth of the eyes made Castle feel like a small boy in the presence of a mystical power.

—You have color in your face, — she said.

—Where is the old man? Did he bring me here? —

She piled the grass in a corner. She approached him. She said,

—You know runa simi. While you slept, you talked in many tongues. —

She felt his forehead, pulled his eyelids up. With one hand, she forced his mouth open. She said,

—Good, you are almost well. —

Castle knew those fingers, had felt them, gentle, curing fingers.

She went to the door, made a clicking noise and the qoy came squealing back to attack the grass.

—He comes soon, — she said. –You rest. Tomorrow you walk. —

She backed him to the edge of the bed until he was sitting again and then she turned and stirred the pot with a wooden spoon. Squatting, she plucked a qoy from the herd and whacked it. There was a pop. The animal was dead. She laid it on the floor and repeated the killing twice more. Castle knew that motion. It had a timelessness to it. She said,

—Never eat mama qoy. —

Castle said, —How long have I been here? —

She ignored him. She slit the skin from the beasts with a thin blade, gutted them and dropped the fat carcasses into the boiling pot. A handful of small yellow and red potatoes. Four ears of choclo. A large aji. Then, rising, she said,

—He comes. —

Vic carried a bundle of grass that he tossed on the pile covering the qoy who squirted up and continued to feast on the fresh grass. Vic said,

"Gotta fatten those critters up. You eat qoy?"

"I eat anything that doesn't have fur still on it."

"Never heard of eatin the fur, but then lots of folks don't eat qoy once they find out what it is. Same with snake. Taste fine though."

"I don't know if I can bite anything," Castle said.

"Petrona's fixin her special soup but if you can't handle it she'll fix you something soft. You went down hard, son. I was gettin worried, but I knew if I got you back here and she got her hooks into you, you'd come along all right. You had soroche and a couple bugs, I guess, plus whatever else happened to you."

"She cured the pain," Castle said.

"She sweated all that out of you. She can cure anything you got. Does it bother you having a witch tend your wounds?"

"She got rid of the swelling."

"Yep. Petrona's the best in the cordillera," Vic said. "She knows everything from how to fix up a sick qoy to how to make a woman have twins. She put that powder on your face only it wasn't power then. It was some kind of Petrona goop, but the swellin came down like a leaky balloon."

"How long was I out?"

"Off and on for two days, but you wasn't here even when you was."

"Vic, I want to go back Quillomayu."

"Yeah, well, they get hold of you again, you don't come out in one piece."

"I'm going to have to kill Jacobs."

Vic sat on the bed and scratched his chin. He said,

"I think you still got the soroche. You think killing him's a good idea? Why don't we stay here for a day or two more and let Petrona wipe out the rest of what's feasting in you?"

"What if he goes back to New York?"

"I'm thinking your head ain't working right. You keep kicking like a chicken you won't get nowhere."

What Vic said made sense.

Castle was still weak. Even standing was hard. Moving made him lightheaded. That was the soroche. If he got to Quillomayu and ran into Jacobs, it wouldn't work. Vic said,

"I was thinking about this tale you told me. There's a couple things I don't get. For one, this Everett didn't seem to get along with Jacobs and Cathay, I mean if killing him is a measure of something like that."

"They were after the same thing."

"But he come outta New York, right?"

"Yes. But Cathay was glad to get Everett out of their hair..."

"After the same thing? That don't make a lotta sense. Everett's mixed up with ol' Villareal and Jacobs and Cathay don't take to that? Maybe. But now I been watching this set up unwind out there with Jacobs' bunch at Quillomayu but I ain't seen no part of Villareal and his bunch out there, in fact, ain't never heard of Villareal being around there."

"You know Villareal?"

"I do, but it's no surprise to me that he don't show up 'cause he never set foot on a piece of unpaved ground in his life. Mud would make him cry. He ain't the kind to go out of his way and neither would you if you just had to snap open your mouth and there was some Indian nanny to stick ceviche in you. The last time he lifted a finger was to pick his nose…"

"I could see that in him. And the woman?"

"What woman?"

"Marta."

"Marta. Whoa, pard. Now there's a mystery if they ever was one. Anyways, what I'm saying is that whatever you think you got going, it ain't what you think it is if you think it's something you know."

Petrona, hunkered down in front of the fire, stirred the pot. Some qoy still nibbled grass, others had closed their eyes and fallen asleep. Castle said,

"This isn't your fight, Vic. It's simple. I want to kill Jacobs. I don't care about the rest…"

"You don't care?"

"Look what he did to me." Castle bared his gums, rubbed his face. "I don't owe him. I want him dead and rotting in a shallow grave after dogs gnaw his bones."

"What's the big picture here? There's things that go way past a little blood vengeance."

"Two people, Vic—the woman and Everett. And how many others? These guys think they can get away with it because they've got the green."

"And what'll that get you? Cuttin'em down?"

Castle pursed his lips—like Vic. He scratched his chin—like Vic. He closed one eye—mimicking Vic as his chameleon genes kicked in and he became the color of the surroundings. He said,

"I owe you, Vic. A lot. For you I listen. Tell me what to do."

"Look at it like this," Vic said. "Villareal and his bunch own half this cordillera and everything in it and what grew on it. I never knew the old man, but when he died, young Villareal was too fay to hang on to it. You gotta be a macho asshole in this country or they walk all over you and hang you by your nuts. Now, what Villareal's got left, won't grow much besides chuño, so they got to get what they can outta what they got."

Castle said, "Villareal doesn't look like the kind who'd give a damn about farming potatoes."

"And he don't. But if what I hear's right, he's in money trouble. Big money. They used to call it land rich, cash poor. That kind that don't go away. That scrawny little son of a bitch likes to spend'er, that much I know."

"And along comes Centrex with a sweetheart deal that will end his worries…"

"And leave him without one hectare. Only Villareal double-crosses Everett with you sitting right there to hear it, and he weasels out of the deal. But what's he got that Everett wants? Huh?"

"And the next day, Everett ends up dead," Castle said.

Vic shifted his weight on the bed. A far-away look in his eyes and he squirted a stream of tobacco juice out the door. Castle pursed his lips and shot a wad at the opening, but his spit hung up after half a meter and plopped on the floor. Petrona said,

—You go outside next time. — She did not smile.

"Takes some practice, son," Vic said. "You're better'n some, but I been doing that for thirty years."

"The big picture, Vic."

"If that'd been snoose, she'd of whipped your ass with that broom over there."

"The question is why did Villareal back out, isn't it?"

"Um huh. Ask what's in it to make Villareal renege on a sure thing? You don't renege if you got money problems which means that sudden-like, he ain't concerned and that makes a man wonder, don't it? How smart are you, son?"

"I can put on my boots without instructions," Castle said.

"Okay. What the hell were they going to mine that Centrex was interested in that Villareal had?"

"They didn't talk about mining anything, only money."

"Those folks at Centrex know something or they don't go around offering Villareal a bundle for his pile of rock when they could steal it just as easy. You know the Spaniards took all the easy swag their first time through—gold, silver, anything shiny. Ever since then it's been pure hell to get anything of value out of this ground and somehow it makes my heart sing to see these Centrex people doing to Villareal what his people done to the Indians."

"How do you know so much about Villareal?"

"Look around you, son, and ask the Indians. I know this—anything gets built in this country, the Indian builds it. A camion might haul a load, but you can bet your bottom dollar that an Indian loaded it at one end and an Indian unloaded it at the other. If there's a rock that needs carrying, it's on the back of that Indian. If there's a road somebody wants to cut, it's the Indian that cuts it. And what do they get for it? Nothing. It ain't even their country to give away. And nobody asks them what they want to do with stuff that's under their feet. Nobody. They might look dumb and maybe they don't know a hell of a lot, but if you want to know something ask one of'em cause one of'em was there doing it. They'll tell you if you ask'em right. Not much else to do but talk and work and one of the things they're talking about is that some outfit is high-gradin a lot of Villareal's holdings and shippin it across the border to the port headed for China. And what's not being high-graded he's sellin off..."

"So why did this operation wind down?" Castle said.

Vic said, "I guess I gave you a bit more than you asked for, huh?"

"How's a man to know unless someone tells him?"

"Sure makes a man wonder what Jacobs botched up, don't it or whether he got to Villareal and turned his head before you and Everett even got here."

Vic puckered up to spit.

"'Course if you kill Jacobs, you won't ever find out, will you?"

The stream of tobacco juice arched through the door and landed outside. Vic squinted, his face hard, the lines deep as gullies in a desert landscape. He said,

"They been working this out piece by piece and I know for certain that the only people that's going to hurt is the Indian. That's the way it always happens…"

Vic looked at Petrona. He said,

—That soup smells good, carita. — Petrona smiled at him.

"Jacobs' thing was the election," Castle said.

"Something's up," Vic said. "You must of seen 'em down in Huañuscacuchu. Last time I was down there, the Nacionales was thick as maggots in llama dung. And Vargas's got a nose like a hound when it comes to the political infight. Problem is that everybody's killing everybody these days. Ever since Vargas took over the Nacionales they been that way."

"And Jacobs' mercenaries?" Castle said.

Vic looked at Castle. Took a breath. Shifted the chaw in his mouth. He said,

"Don't know much about 'em but the Nacionales? I seen them bastards cut the legs off a man with those machine pistols they tote around and not say shit or how do you do. That's not how it was when old Villareal was the caudillo. The Nacionales then was kind of like big old dumb puppy dogs."

"Old Villareal. The father?"

"That's right. He was the caudillo before the families took over."

"The families?"

"What interests me right now is that notebook."

"Why the notebook?"

"What do you figure Everett was using that thing for?"

"He didn't talk about it."

"Well, I'd speculate that it's got something to do with his business up here, wouldn't you? He had it when you were up at Tarma?"

"Yes. In the briefcase."

"Records of some kind?"

"Maybe."

"Maybe hell, boy. You're so dumb you probably hurt when you sleep. Think about it. He keeps this notebook. He don't let you see it. All of a sudden he's dyin, he hands it to you, and you think it's your ordinary everyday address book? You know now you wasn't 'sposed to let Cathay get his meathooks on it since he's the one who did in ol' Everett, so what are you supposed to do with it?"

"Huh," Castle muttered.

"Jesus H. Christ, Castle. Everett weren't no dummy. He wanted you bad but from what I can tell you ain't all that worth having but I ain't Everett, I don't go putting numbers in a little book, so you must be good for something so what it is?"

Castle let Vic's tirade go by. He'd never thought of just why Everett wanted him. But he was beginning to see that maybe Vic was right.

Vic shot a stream of tobacco juice out the door.

Petrona finished the soup. She stood. The guinea pigs chattered around her feet, but she didn't pay them any mind.

"All right now. You need some rest and a little bit of Petrona's medicine. You hungry?"

"I could eat."

—Petrona, this boy wants some of that witch's brew and you better let him have some of that soup before he faints on us again. —

Petrona handed Castle the cup full of a silvery liquid and then she sprinkled a white powder on top of it. It floated, then disappeared. Castle said,

—Kuka? —

—Ari,— Petrona said. —Drink it, you'll feel better. —

Castle sipped the brew, a sharp taste, tangy, like wild flower tea.

She ladled soup into a metal bowl. The qoy had cooked, the potatoes were soft, the choclo sweet. Petrona said,

—After you eat, you sleep. —

—You better believe you'll sleep, — Vic said.

FIFTEEN

Vic had taken Petrona to deliver a baby leaving Castle with the guinea pigs, his broken teeth, and notebook. When Vic came in he tossed his hat on the bed, ladled some soup from the pot that was cold because Castle had let the fire go out. He said,

"You let the fire go out. Petrona will have your head."

"Sorry," Castle said. "I got into the notebook."

"How's the arm?" Vic said. He sucked the meat off the bones and ate the potatoes with his fingers.

"The stuff Petrona fed me killed everything almost."

"Ought to. That's powerful medicine, that kuka mix she puts together. You say you got into the notebook?"

Castle spread a page of the notebook. Vic picked it up. He said,

"Can't read it, too small."

"Everett wrote in minuscule so you can't read it without a glass."

"But you can read it?"

"I can read it some," Castle said. "Lithium."

"That makes you dangerous, don't it? Knowing what's in it?"

Vic finished his soup, took a bit of his tobacco plug. and said,

"Lithium?"

"Lithium."

The old man squinted at Castle then puckered his lips. With no teeth, his mouth tightened with deep lines running from the lips out, forming an exotic flower of flesh. His tongue darted from the center, snake-like. He said,

"All right. If you say so. Lithium."

"Everett sort of coded to make anyone trying to figure it out go crazy."

"What does it say? The little writing, what does it say?"

"He didn't write in whole sentences, Vic. It's kind of a shorthand. For instance, of writing Villareal he uses V. And the numbers."

"Words that you can't read, numbers that don't mean nothing."

"I can almost read'em."

"Then what's it say?"

"It's a kinda telegraphic writing, pappy."

"Telegraphic writing?"

"I don't know," Castle said. "The only way you really know what it's about is to ask Everett but he's dead."

"So you don't know what it says."

"I do know what it says, kind of...Everett was the most secretive man I've ever met. He didn't want to tell you his name. To tell the truth, I'm not sure his name was Everett Richards. I think he was paying bribes. He was trying to buy whatever it was and I think it was lithium. In Tarma, Villareal and Everett talked about tonnage and price per ton. All the numbers with Ks are bribes."

"Who was he bribin? Jacobs? Villareal?"

"Everett found out that Jacobs and Cathay were into something together and that's why he was killed. I think the deal with Villareal was a decoy."

"What do you mean by decoy?"

"In the notebook, Everett writes that Jacobs had betrayed Centrex. Nothin else. There was a safe in the office where the woman was killed. There were disks with some kind of data on them, but they were gone. Here's what I get from the notebook—There's a name that starts with a V. It ain't Villareal. The numbers Everett wrote was V 250k. That's it. The only name with just a V."

"A name? there's a lot of names that start with V. Villareal, Vega, Vazquez, Velazquez, Valenzuela, Vargas."

"Any of that mean anything to you, Vic?"

"Vargas," Vic said.

"What if it ain't a last name at all?" Castle said. "I think it's a name beginnin' with V and the k means thousand, but what if it means twenty-five thousand... men."

"Men?" Vic said.

"Argentinos, Chilenos, Venezolanos, Mexicanos..."

"Is that in there?"

"I think it's all about an army of mercenaries, Vic. I saw them out there at the campamento in Quillomayu. Everett, he was carrying a ton of cash in that briefcase. All those little ks means he was payin off a lot of people with a lotta cash. But why? Everett was a Centrex man, so I gotta think that whatever he was doin it was for Centrex. Now Everett had his fixation with secrecy. He didn't want anyone, even me, knowin what he was doin and that's why he goes'n puts all that in code. On the night he wrote that V 250k, he told me to go out. Now if V is a person, it tells me a couple of things. For one, he was meetin' this V alone and two V speaks English."

"That's the long way around the mountain," Vic said.

"It's simple, Pappy. Everett's got this mania for knowing what people were sayin', cause he's all the time thinkin' that folks gotta be talkin 'bout him so he drags me along so's I can let him know what they's sayin. Since he's not gonna meet without a interpreter, the person he's meetin spoke English. Villareal don't speak English. All we have to do's find someone whose name, first or last, starts with V and who speaks English."

"Well that sort of limits it to maybe two or three million people."

"There's two names in this here notebook that reach out and grab you by the nuts. One of them's Llapa Atipac and the other's Quillomayu."

"I'll be gutted and boiled," Vic said. "Llapa Atipac."

"You know what Llapa Atipac is?"

"Do I know what Llapa Atipac is?"

"Maybe the whole thing ain't lithium though lithium sure as snot is part of it, but the real thing is that military bunch out there in Quillomayu—why?"

Vic got up to spit, but just as he stood, the guinea pigs stampeded out of the room and Vic turned blue holding the spit, but then he let it go and his timing was off and instead of heading out the door, the glob of tobacco juice splatted just inside.

"What's Llapa Atipac?" Castle said.

"Llapa Atipac, the all powerful...."

"I know what it means," Castle said, "what is it?"

"There's been chatter for years that there was uranium out there. The ones that denied it's probably the same ones that didn't think there was oil in the Oriente til the Ecuadorians hit their bonanza."

"What's it mean if there's uranium at Llapa Atipac?"

"It'd mean somebody's gonna wanna mine it."

"Everett was talking about mining with Villareal."

"Llapa Atipac is what's left of Villareal's patrimonio."

"And we know that Quillomayu is connected to Cathay and there's nothing to keep us from thinking that V is connected either to Cathay and his secret army or to Villareal and his uranium."

"You're tryin to hook up papaya to qoy turds, son."

"Everett ran into something. 'Spose he gets to payin off someone in Cathay's organization so as to protect Centrex's aims—whatever they are…?"

"And maybe Llapa Atipac and Quillomayu mean something together, but how in hell does uranium hook up to lithium?"

"Maybe Cathay makes an offer to Villareal that Everett don't got a chance in hell to match."

"Nah. You left Villareal in Tarma turnin down Everett's money, so wouldn't be money."

"Right. Wouldn't be money. Course there's only a coupla things you can use uranium for. What's more powerful that money, Vic?"

"Well, if you put it that way and you got Quillomayu and Llapa Atipac together, you get a bomb."

"That don't make a whole lotta sense, does it? Everett's got fingers in both Quillomayu and Llapa Atipac, but if he's hooked up with Cathay and Jacobs, and Jacobs has betrayed Centrex, why does Cathay have Everett killed."

"You don't know that he did," Vic said.

"Cathay knows where Everett's goin when he goes to Tarma, but what Everett was after was so big that not even Jacobs, the head of Centrex Security knew about it…."

"He didn't know because Everett didn't put it in the notebook."

"And Cathay didn't know nothin about the notebook. And now, who is Jacobs workin for if he's not workin for Centrex??

"Cathay."

"And who is Cathay working for?"

"Whoever put up the money to steal Quillomayu from Villareal."

"And that's not Centrex," Castle said.

Castle stopped. He was tired.

The qoy came back inside to continue their attack on the grass. Vic tugged at his tobacco plug. Waiting. Castle said,

"Wish I had a man to ask about all this. Cathay knows, Jacobs knows, but I can't talk to them cause they see me, I'm dead."

"'Bout the only man you can talk to ain't talking a whole lot."

"Well shit, Vic. We don't know who this V is, but we sure as hog snot know who Villareal is."

Vic squinted, puckered up and squirted a stream of juice out the door. He sniffled. Then said,

"You're crazy, boy. I been around you long enough to think I know what you're thinkin."

"Spose, just 'spose of a sec we go talk to Villareal and knowin what we know, get him to tell us what he knows about this whole thing and what it's about."

"And he's gonna tell you."

"It won't hurt to ask. I've been running. What if I quit running, turn around and jam this straight down their throats?"

"How you gonna get to Villareal? You just got through tellin me Cathay wants you dead and he's got the man on your tail so you're just gonna roll in there lookin like a long lost Indio from who knows where the hell from and he's gonna open up like a Vegas jackpot."

"Can you think of another way?" Castle said.

"You know, I kinda like you cause I got a soft spot for idiots and somebody's gotta look out for idiots. But this Jacobs ain't your casual playmate. He likes to kill people just to watch'em piss their pants when they die. So before you go divin off the deep end, back off and say this ain't none of your business."

Castle stopped, took a deep breath, looked at Vic. He said,

"That son of a bitch kicked my teeth in, Vic. He'd have beaten my brains out…"

"And you're gonna change all that, how?"

"I don't want to change it, pappy. I just want to kill Jacobs and maybe get some revenge for Everett. I guess you can say I want to get even."

"You're a vindictive little bastard, ain't ya?"

"Can you get me back to Huañuscacuchu?"

"Face it, son, you go to Huañuscacuchu you don't stand a chance in hell of livin a week."

"You been here for thirty years, Vic. You know the cordillera."

Vic sucked his chaw in silence, squinting and making noises with his puckered lips. He said,

"I can get you there but it'll take a while cause you got Nacionales and Jacobs and his militia after you so we'll have to go over the border and come in through Ipiales with all the smugglers. I done it before."

SIXTEEN

Vic's Land Rover circled the fountain twice, each time passing the Café Montmartre, each time looking like a wounded dinosaur hunting a herd of gazelles.

When the vehicle lumbered around for its third pass, Castle left the table on Avenida Marechal Foch, and, folding the newspaper, walked down to Calle Santa Maria.

It was a narrow street lined with low stone fences. Castle waited in a gateway until Vic made the turn, lurched to a stop, got out, opened the hood and pulled at wires while muttering to himself.

Castle glanced back at Avenida Marechal Foch where traffic continued to flow past. No Nacionales in jeeps, none of Cathay's khaki-shirted fascists.

Vic closed the hood as Castle come to him. He said,

"I was getting worried."

"It ain't easy for me to play this game, son. I can't seem to get the hang of it the way you do. My daddy taught me to tell the truth, so that might have something to do with it."

"Did you find Villareal?"

"Not there. Talked to the sister."

"Didn't know he had a sister."

"Course even if she'd of told me somethin, I might not of understood cause she talks like she grew a mouthful of cotton."

"Castilian," Castle said.

"Castilian?"

"Yeah, turns the S to Th so Castilian comes out Cathtilian. Spanish dialect."

"See? You know all sortsa stuff."

Castle tapped the newspaper on the hood of the jeep. He said,

"I don't know what's going on, Pappy. Paper's got Villareal saying he might run for president."

"Kinda late, ain't it?'

"I've got to talk to him, Vic."

"What's goin on in that rat's nest you call a brain?"

"I want to be in that house when he comes back."

"Don't know how wise that'll be, son."

"If I were wise, pappy, I'd have stayed in New York to do my hunting."

"How do you reckon to get in there?"

"You ever see a worm get into an apple?"

*****

The bars on the windows were elaborate, wrought iron, and painted black. The room they guarded was cold, tiled, the walls uncovered like the walls of a prison cell.

Castle opened the glass doors that looked out onto the street. He saw Vic in the Rover a few doors down. Darkness was closing over him. In the seat, beside him, a

Nacional sat trussed up like an aging athlete's hernias. Satisfied, Castle closed the doors and returned to the desk with its big leather chair. The chair squeaked as he sat, a yowl of unoiled springs broke out in the room. Castle stood, brushed his hand over his pant legs as if to see that the brown stains on the chair which grew fungus-like on the leather had seeped onto him.

In the hour he had waited, he had counted the stains. Some were wine, others dark as blood, some the unmistakable smears of semen.

Castle listened to the sounds of the house—servants moving downstairs, doing what they did when no one was watching. In the immensity of the dwelling, they were not to be heard. An occasional door closing spoke to the isolation.

Onorato, surprise on his face, had met him at the side gate of the house. Jumping at the sight of the uniform, he smiled when he saw Castle. He said.

—Ah! Castle! —He opened the gate with one of the keys on his majordomo ring. –You are not my cousin and so you do not bring news from my village. But I knew this because I have no cousins who are Nacionales. —Castle said,

—I need your help, my friend. —

—Because of the dead gringo? —

Onorato checked the street before closing the gate.

—You know about him? —

—Everyone in Huañuscacuchu knows. —

—But you alone know I did not kill him. —

—It elates me that you escaped,— Onorato said. –When I heard, I worried, because I know what the Nacionales do. What help do you need? —

—I need to talk to the patron. —

—He is away. —-

—I can wait. —

—You have been hurt. —Onorato said. Your face, your mouth, your teeth—

He grasped Castle's arm.

—I have been hurt. More than it shows. —

—Something terrible is happening in Ayahuantu, —Onorato said.

—It does not go well. It concerns Don Eduardo. —

Onorato slumped. He released Castle's arm. He said,

—That is so, my brother. There are men who would now do great evil. There is a story I learned yesterday about a man who upon learning about the dictatorship, arose each morning, ate his breakfast without talking to anyone—not his wife, nor his children, not his servants—went back to bed. On the day he learned that Vargas had set himself up as dictator for life, he ate his breakfast, added a peeled banana that he ate with a knife and fork then shot himself in the head. His body disappeared. —

—Why have you told me this, my brother? —

—It tells us what will happen. Soon. And Don Eduardo is not innocent. —

—Yes. He is in the middle of it somehow. —

—You would not come here for yourself. You know something, — Onorato said.

—It is a dangerous time, — Castle said, —but I mean him no harm. —

—He is a child, Castle. He understands nothing. He does not understand what these men ask of him. —

—Is he serious about the presidency? —

—He is serious about nothing. That is why I must protect him. —

—I wish I had friends as loyal as you, Onorato. —

—You do. Let me show you to your room. —

The room overlooked the street. Onorato told Castle he would come for him when the patron came home. Onorato locked the door behind him. A precaution, he said.

*****

Villareal returned after midnight. Castle watched a taxi stop in front of the house and honk its horn. Twice.

The street remained empty except for the Land Rover with Vic and the half-naked Nacional.

Villareal was not followed, was not surveilled. That puzzled Castle. Villareal had said he wanted to be president, but he had no protection, no bodyguard.

The taxi door opened. The little man stepped out. A woman followed. Not Marta.

Castle watched Villareal walk. In the light of the street, he seemed bent, like an old man. Castle heard Onorato open the front door, then the gate in the fence. He heard the woman's heels click on the pavement, then on the steps.

She laughed.

Then there was silence.

*****

Waiting for Onorato, Castle was impatient. He had promised he would wait, but he did not wait well. He went to the balcony but held up. Another way in? No. He had told Onorato he would wait for him to come. He had to wait. He had given his word.

He came alert when the door opened and the majordomo slipped in, his finger to his lips. Silence.

—It is late, my friend, the patron is...—

—In flagrante? —Castle said.

—The woman with him. How can you talk to him? —

—Tonight, Onorato, tonight. It has to be. —

—I did not know they could come. They are his weakness. —

—As they are mine. —

78

—I remember. I will take you in but please, he must not know...—

—I will tell him nothing, friend. He will see me, but he will not think of you. —

Onorato led Castle into a darkened hallway. The only announcement was a faint creaking of the ancient wooden floor.

*****

Villareal clinging to the woman's naked back was a tiny white parasite.

She grunted.

She groaned.

Groans punctuated Villareal's high-pitched wails as the woman, undulating called out, —Ay papito! Ay papito!—

Castle, in the doorway, swung the door into the wall with a crack.

The woman tilted her head toward the sound.

Villareal jerked up.

Villareal still wore his dark glasses. His pointed beard, flecked with saliva, gave him the puzzled if degenerate look of an aging satyr coupling with a nymph while the woman, on her hands and knees, was all black flowing hair and mythic brown flesh. She was ancient.

Castle surveyed them. An ordinary man might have backed away but it didn't concern him to see Villareal with his decorum violated.

The room was enormous. The bed was littered with satin pillows. A library on one wall went from floor to ceiling. A large carved desk with heavy leather and carved wooden chairs.

On the wall by the street window there was a collection of swords, daggers, and pistols, an array for armor.

Castle knew he was safe. He glanced for a second longer at an epée.

—Castle! —Villareal croaked. –Have you come to kill me too? —

The woman lurched, unseating her rider, sending him onto his back, legs dangling over the edge of the bed. She rolled, pulling the sheet with her.

Villareal's voice changed from a croak to a squeak. He straightened his dark glasses.

—Should I? —

—You speak Castellano? —Villareal said.

— Tell her to dress and go. —

—This surprises me, — Villareal said. –Finding you in the middle of the night in my bedroom wearing the uniform of the Nacionales. —

—That I am alive surprises you? — Castle said.

—Marta did not tell me you know Castellano. —

Villareal laughed. He clasped his hands together. Got off the bed. He said,

—So you know everything. —

Castle walked to the bed. He pulled the sheet from the woman, then picked up the dress that lay on the floor. She smelled of cigars and whiskey, she smelled of perfume and semen. She was slender, large breasted, a body that didn't match the face which wore a heavy covering of makeup, the lips laden with red lipstick, the corners of her mouth puckered and tight, the ravages of her oral arts. Castle admired the decadent lushness of her, the putty-soft bearing of a lifetime spent on her back or on her knees with her mouth open. Castle measured her eyes and her nose and he knew she was pure. He said in Quechua,

—What is your name, my love? —

—Eufemia—she answered.

—Have you received your money? —

—Yes. –

—Put on your dress and leave. They will call a taxi for you. —

Eufemia put on the emerald dress. No underwear. She stepped into strapless green high heels. She looked at Castle, questioning tempered with fear. Castle said,

—Go, now. —

He heard the clicks of heels in the hall, down the stairway, heard Onorato speaking to her and then silence. Castle turned to Villareal.

—This is most unusual, — Villareal said. –I find it vaguely amusing like something from Lope. Do you know Lope? –

Villareal giggled, made a cross while sliding his finger across his throat as if it were a dagger.

—Yes, I know Lope, but I am here because my only interest in you is to help myself. —

—Is it money you wish? It's certainly not women you want. —

—I wish to know about Llapa Atipac. —

—There is nothing to know about Llapa Atipac. —

Castle turned to the cold voice washing over him. His eyes searched the wall, landing on the sabre.

She stood in the doorway in black—black yoga pants, black scoop-neck. Tight. Black round-toe flats. Her hair that luminescent white. Castle felt a pain like a hot coal in his groin. Not fear. Not anger. But the sight of her set fire to his own hidden limits. Frozen, he could not look away from her. She had used him without any thought for his pleasure and she had discarded him when her own had been gratified. How could she, after that, draw his fire so fast, so hard at a time when there was no time. And now, she looked at him as if seeing him for the first time.

She closed the door.

Castle let his breath work against the pain in his chest.

He had to drive the passion down, had to think. Not sex now, but a challenge.

She circled Castle until she stood between him and Villareal.

—I think there is something to know, — Castle said. A victory—his voice did not break. Did not quaver. –And I think it's linked to Everett's death. —

"I know nothing about Everett's death." Marta's eyes peered into Castle inventorying his pain, correlating it to some diagram she had in her head. Castle remembered her on the bed. Once you've had someone, no matter what the having amounted to, could you ever forget or say no?

—I must interject, — Villareal said. –Marta is not merely an interpreter, as your departed patron Don Everett seemed to think, but she is what in chivalric days my great, great grandfather would have called his confidante, his companion in all things. She knows everything I know, sir, and if she says there is nothing to know about Llapa Atipac, whatever Llapa Atipac is, who are we to argue? May I offer you a drink, sir? –

—It's the property you were negotiating in Tarmac. —

—No, — Marta said.

—Yes, — Villareal said.

—Tell him nothing, Eduardo, he is a wanted man, you owe him nothing. —

Villareal stood on the bed, staring, now, defiance in his eyes, over Marta. He said,

—She is right. Given that I owe you no explanation, given that I can lift the phone and have you thrown into that miserable Vargas' prison in an instant. I find your presence boring, exhausting, unspeakable and impudent. This is, after all, my bedroom and it is the middle of the night and you are a wanted criminal. —

Castle walked to the wall of weapons, seized the sabre from its scabbard. With a single sweep of the blade, he hewed a lamp in half and without a flinch, powered the sabre through the back of one leather chair, splitting it. Then, hurling the sabre like a lance, stuck it into the wall then stood, hands on hips, looking at the man with two heads. Villareal said, his voice rising to a guttural whisper,

—On the other hand, Marta, my dear, perhaps you are acting in haste by not telling this man what he wants to know. —

—Don't be a fool, Eduardo. —

Villareal climbed off the bed making conciliatory gestures to Castle. He was naked except for the open white shirt that was spotted with lipstick. He scurried to the desk that stood in front of the wall of weapons, glanced at the scabbard and ran his fingers over the sliced-open leather chair. He said,

—You used my great great grandfather's sabre. He was an alferez real. —

Villareal sat in the ornate chair, curled his feet under him like a Buddha, then drew an enormous cigar from a wooden box and lit it. He said,

—Here is a man, Marta. Look at him. He looks like a toothless cholito—no teeth, his face a mess. But he is a warrior and he has evaded the devils of that son of a whore we call a minister of security. —

He glanced at Marta.

—Now," Villareal said, —you are not impressed, but here is a man who, until a short time ago, we did not know existed, yet here he is with us in my bedroom. That is the feat of a great warrior, Marta. Look at him. —

—Eduardo, —Marta said, —shut your stupid little mouth. —

—Clearly this is no ordinary man, Marta. While running from the Nacionales and the second-rate thief Ricardo Cathay and his team of killers, he has found out about Llapa Atipac. —

—And Quillomayu,— Castle said.

—Ay! Quillomayu. You see, Marta. We have a champion in the room. What a man. —

—Quillomayu,— Castle said.

—Llapa Atipac has been a cancer on my family for generations. It is a useless desert. —

Marta stiffened. She crossed her arms over her breasts. She looked like a black insect, her white head protruding from its carapace. Villareal said,

—You see, Castle, Marta my lovely who has a fetish for aliens doesn't want me to tell you about Llapa Atipac or Quillomayu. But why shouldn't I tell you everything? You can't tell anyone because you will not leave here. —

—Is there uranium at Llapa Atipac? —Castle said.

—Uranium? I shit on uranium. Lithium. —

Villareal left the chair and jumped up on the desk, peering into Castle's eyes. He said,

—Yes, Yes to everything. Even with lithium Llapa Atipac is worthless. It is dung. Other men were bequeathed vast pampas, cattle, castles, fortunes in gold, but what was I bequeathed? What did my degenerate father leave me? Lithium. And Vargas, that devil. And a sister who bullies me and fornicates with her aliens. Llapa Atipac and lithium. Imagine, Castle, your father shitting a gigantic turd and leaving it to you for your future—that is Llapa Atipac. One thousand six hundred hectares that will not even grow potatoes. What good is ground that won't grow potatoes? Ground on which cattle die? I do not understand this. —

Castle glanced at Marta, still sculpted in black, arms folded, mouth hard, eyes narrow. Castle said,

"He doesn't know."

"Of course not," Marta said. "He is a little fool."

—English, — Villareal said. – Fucking English. I should have learned English. —

"You know."

"Yes, I know."

—And yet, — Villareal said, —men are willing to pay large sums of money for land that will not even grow corn. —

"Cathay?" Castle said.

"He has made a tender."

"And Everett?"

"Second best. Not enough."

—What are you two plotting? —Villareal said.

—Go lie down, Eduardo, — Marta said. —I'll let you know in the morning. —

"What are they doing out at Quillomayu?" Castle said.

"Nothing."

"Why are there troops out there?"

"There are no Nacionales at Quillomayu."

"Troops. Armed men. Not Nacionales."

—What about Nacionales? — Villareal said. – Marta?—

—Eduardo, these are things you don't need to worry about. Go lie down. You've had a hard time. Go rest. —

—No. —Villareal said.

"Who does Cathay represent and who gives him the resources to develop Quillomayu?"

—You have ruined a perfectly good chair, Castle, — Villareal said. —I will hate your forever for that. It came from my great great grandfather and my own father sat there when he made decisions about the lives of these Ayahuantuan peasants and you have cut it in half. —

"An American company," Marta said.

"What is he building at Chacanahuayco?"

—Quillomayu, Chacanahuayco, Llapa Atipac. Marta. What is all this about? — Villareal got down off the desk and took his place on the desk chair.

—Get on the bed, Eduardo. Close your eyes. —

Castle went to the window. Saw Vic standing in the street. Castle said,

—What did Jacobs mean when he said wait until after the election? —

—Election, — Villareal said. —I am the candidate, but she will be president. I sit at the desk and get my picture taken, but Marta...—

Villareal lay his head on the desk and he was asleep.

Marta smiled. It wasn't a lover's smile, but a hard and deep and ugly smile.

"Is that so?" Castle said. He glanced again at the street where he saw Vic, talking to Jacobs. Castle froze. Vic talking to Jacobs, Jacobs nodding and looking up at the window.

Castle backed away, turning to Marta, the rush of adrenalin jangling his nerves.

Marta said, —They are here for you, Castle. You are a dead man. —

—You called Jacobs? You're working with Jacobs? And Vic? —

—Chacanahuayco. For making the strike, he takes five percent of the gross. —

Castle ran to the sabre stuck in the wall and yanked it out and turned to the sleeping Villareal.

Marta said, —Don't. He's nothing. Nothing but a name. —

—And Cathay? —

Marta came up to him, placed her hand on the sabre. She said, —You know too much already. —

Castle jumped at the sound of hammering on the door downstairs. Onorato.

Castle went into the corridor. He shouted, —Onorato. —

Onorato appeared in the atrium. He looked up.

—Onorato, — Marta said, —open the door. —

—Don't open it, Onorato, — Castle shouted.

—Open the door, Onorato. —

She tried to push past Castle, but he caught her and threw her to the floor.

—Onorato, — Marta screamed, —open the door you stupid animal, open the door or I'll have your head. —

Castle stood over her, raised the sabre. She grinned at him, teeth like razors. Castle hesitated, then he clipped her on the chin with the guard of the sabre and, still holding the sabre, dashed down the stairs.

Pounding the door. Shouts.

—This is the end, Onorato, — Castle said. —I have to get out of here. —

—Come, — Onorato said.

He led Castle through the house, through the kitchen, outside. He shoved Castle and he said,

—This was the stable. —

Castle skidded through another doorway.

There was a rush of footsteps.

Marta had opened the door. Jacobs and his men were in.

Castle crouched, still with the sabre, then rising and swinging the sabre like a hammer, he broke bone, yowl of pain, a machine pistol fired, its muzzle lighting the darkness for a second.

—Castle, — Onorato calling. —Here.—

Hands clawing at him, Castle thrust with the sabre, blood, another yell then Castle pierced a body and the blade met bone and Onorato called him.

Castle felt a hand on his leg. He dropped to his knees hacking with the sabre and then, the air was filled with its peculiar odor and there was dust.

Onorato opened a gate. Castle hoisted himself to his feet. Onorato shoved him, —Go. Go. Quickly. —

Castle grasped the majordomo by the arm, and tried to pull him along, but Onorato broke free. Castle then ran. And ran, and as he ran, he heard gunshots behind him. Nowhere near him and he knew he was free.

He turned a corner and ran into a sudden panic. He was looking into the gun barrels of a cluster of Nacionales. Behind the Nacionales, he saw Jacobs and beside Jacobs he saw Vic. He raised the sabre. Too late. He dropped it.

Nowhere to go this time.

SEVENTEEN

He woke up. He didn't know what had happened. His hair was matted against his head. He stank of sweat and urine. There was blood on his arm.

Eyes closed, he hunched down in a corner, his back against a wall.

A sound caught his ear. He opened his eyes. His heart beat faster. His breath came in gasps. His chest hurt. His lungs ached. His throat was raw.

He quivered.

He blinked. His eyes hurt.

But his door didn't open.

He again closed his eyes as he listened to the now familiar shuffling sound.

He relaxed.

The sound was the muffled sound of someone being dragged.

It was a welcome sound because it meant they were not coming for him.

He would have smiled at the reprieve, but he had forgotten how.

He pushed himself erect.

He was slope-shouldered with pain and dizzy from hunger.

When he moved, he hobbled, unable to avoid touching the soles of his bare feet. His feet were black with dirt and bruises and the bruises were hard lumps.

He took a step. Small smears of blood stained the floor. But there were others. And his arm.

The shuffling faded to an eerie silence. Sound, here, did not travel well, but muffled, fettered, it acted as though once loose, it could not escape.

A door opened. Closed. The jangle of keys. The shuffling now came back.

The sound of the cell door opposite his opening. The sound of the door hitting the wall was a relief. The clatter of keys was a spiritual experience in the deadened atmosphere.

They had brought Talavera back.

Through the small, barred opening, he saw the backs of the two Nacionales. One of them jabbed Talavera in the kidney. Talavera groaned.

Castle winced and sagged but held himself erect.

Then there came a hollow sound, an inhuman gagging, the cry of a being who no longer could scream.

Castle smelled the blood, felt the blows as if they were landing on him.

As the Nacionales backed out of the cell, Castle caught a glimpse of Talavera on the floor, naked, rigid, his penis erect, the electric wire still protruding. His scrotum was swollen and black from the rubber band cinched around the base.

Castle withdrew into quiet when the guards closed the door. As they walked away, they were talking about a small restaurant in Huañuscacuchu where they heard that rich gringas came looking for a macho lover.

—I'll give them a macho cock, — one of them said, —but with the gringas you have to be careful about the disease. —

—Do you ask them if they have it? —

—They all have it. —

—All of them? —

—Use a condom, even if you fuck them in the mouth, you jerk. —

Castle listened to Talavera retching in his cell. When the electric shock tensed the muscles, the body remained rigid for a time. As it relaxed, convulsions ripped through the body, electric inner storms sweeping through the nerves. Castle closed his eyes. When the retching stopped, he whispered,

—Federico? Federico? —

But there was only silence.

Holding his gut, Castle slithered down the wall until he squatted, head hanging between his knees. He was now an animal. He was guilt because he had been lucky. He could, if he had to, speak, but Talavera, when they had dragged the poet from his cell, had called them sons of bitches, sons of whores and priests, shit-eaters, but when he returned, he hadn't uttered one word. They had destroyed his rebellion. They had destroyed him.

Castle knew then the complete and utter meaning of helpless.

They had beaten him too. Without explanations or questions.

Beaten him on the soles of his feet.

In the kidneys.

He pissed blood.

They had beaten him in the face, hammering the already destroyed face. But they had not taken his language.

Federico had not been so lucky.

Under the gray hood chained over his head, the face would be unrecognizable.

Under the hood, the poet no longer existed.

He had ceased to be in his stages of torture.

To end it, they had taken his words.

*****

Then he heard footsteps again. Keys jangling. He tensed. He closed his eyes, tried to locate the part of his brain that shut out what was going to happen. He wanted to deaden his body, to separate the flesh from the pain. Two Nacionales hauled him to his feet, blindfolded him, tied his hands, and dragged him from his cell. He wanted to say no.

He stumbled up a flight of stairs.

No point in asking where he was going.

The cool air surprised him.

Outside.

He shuddered because he knew they were going to kill him—the blindfold, the two guards, outside air meant death.

But, instead, they shoved him into a car.

Still bad. He knew that when they take you away in a car, they are going to kill you. Someone, somewhere would find a corpse with no name. No hands. No face.

Castle resigned himself to his destruction.

The car traveled. The car stopped. The Nacionales pulled him out.

They dragged him up another flight of stairs.

The stone was cold under his bare feet, the boots of the guards echoed.

An elevator.

He was confused, disoriented. He wasn't dead. They wouldn't kill him in an elevator.

A hand gripped his shoulder, shoved him into a chair.

He sat in the quiet. Nothing happened. No one spoke to him. No one hit him.

*****

He heard a door open.

Heard the door close.

His hands were untied, the blindfold removed.

He sat blinking in bright light.

He was in an office. The windows barred. The floor bare. A desk and chair.

His eyes turned to the opening of the door. Entering the room was the Minister of Security, Vargas, chief of the Policia Nacional, a dictator with complete power. Castle was not surprised. Nothing surprised him now. It was natural to see Vargas standing there.

Vargas was a man who commanded respect. He wore military khaki without insignia or name tag. He was taller than he should have been and there was power in his build. Broad shoulders tapered to a thin waist that widened to thick legs that had spent time on mountain slopes carrying burdens. There was no fat in the face, no softness in the belly. The face was an Indian face with high cheekbones and a sculpted nose that put his ancestry into a pure past. Castle, looking at Vargas, wondered just how a man such as he had risen so high.

Vargas studied him. Fixed hard stare that didn't let go until they had stripped out everything there was to know. It was a stare that penetrated exteriors until the truth revealed itself.

From his shirt pocket, Vargas drew a packet of cigarettes—dry, rough, strong cigarettes that, Castle knew, were never the choice of the elite. Vargas offered a cigarette, but Castle said no. He could not fathom what was going on. His hands tingled, he wanted to run. His brain had quit giving him information but flooded him with one directive—run. But there was no exit. Reaching deep into his own past, Castle pushed himself upright. If you can't run, sit straight. Show nothing. Be dumb. Play dead. Vargas said,

—You are more than what I'd heard about you. —

He spoke in Quechua.

—You have an extraordinary talent for being invisible. That is remarkable. This is possible, of course, because you are so completely ordinary. —

Castle felt words birthing in his brain. To his surprise, they came out but not the words he had imagined.

—What about Talavera? —

Talavera. The hoarseness in his throat came out as a croak. His lips, swollen, were thick and alien.

—Talavera. —Vargas said. –This is a small country, small events matter so much. —

—Inga, —Castle said. He felt his brain bringing up one word then forced his voice to speak another. Inga. Why Inga?

—Do you have a purpose, Castle? —

Vargas lit his cigarette. Raw, black tobacco. Castle breathed it in. Took life from it. Vargas said,

—Where do you come from? What is your name? It is not Castle. How have you, in this time, managed to build a wall around yourself so complete no one can penetrate it? This is extraordinary. I would not notice you on the street and I know everything that goes on in Ayahuantu. —

Vargas smoked his cigarette in slow motion. Castle focused on each puff, each trail of smoke.

Vargas said, —You interest me for one reason. Everett. I needed people to think you were Everett's assassin. Your actions were perfect. So listen to me now. —

Snuffing out his cigarette in a metal ashtray, Vargas leaned on the desk.

—You are nothing, yet everyone who can read, knows you are a killer. I am the only being in this country who knows you are not. A lesser man might not be sitting here with me. A lesser man would be stretched out somewhere with a bullet in his brain. You are not a lesser man. You are intelligent and I prize intelligence, real, animal intelligence, and I know that you are intelligent enough to recognize a good deal when you hear it. I'm offering you a deal because I know you can be useful to me. —

Vargas stared, his intensity sweeping over Castle in waves. In the voice, Castle heard truth and he heard power. In the words, there was absolute certainty. There was, of course, a deal and of course, he would accept it, but deeper in Vargas, Castle detected a space for negotiation. He read into the tone of Vargas' speech, a hesitation. Castle said,

—A deal. —

—What is your life worth? —

—Not much. —

—That is correct. I'll let you keep it in return for a small service. —

—In your world, there is no such thing as a small service, — Castle said.

A sentence. A complete sentence. He smiled in his mind, but not with his lips.

—If you accept, you will, in time, be allowed to leave Ayahuantu. If you refuse, you'll go back where you were and you will stay there until someone makes an end to you. —

—Like Talavera. —

Vargas stood. Came around the desk. Leaning over, eyes nailed into Castle, he said,

—Do you live or do you die? —

No negotiation. Castle was wrong. This man was not one to negotiate. He had no need for negotiation. How had Castle read him wrong? His root of power was in balance—he said one thing and always the listener heard something else, and that, Castle knew was not just a gift, but the key—no one could know what Vargas wanted until he already had it. No negotiation.

Vargas called out. The door opened. Two Nacionales at attention, fear in their eyes, hands trembling. Castle felt the power then of the man in front of him. By his presence he brought ordinary men to quiver. He said,

—Back into the hole or out into the sun? —

—Sun, — Castle said.

—Out, — Vargas said.

The Nacionales, given a reprieve, vanished. Vargas sat down at the desk. He smiled. He said,

—I've arranged for you to be put up in Hidalgo. It's a small town a short distance from Huañuscacuchu. There you will wait. Colonel Rodriguez will be with you. Colonel Rodriguez is not a gentle man. He is one of the most efficient killers I know. He will instruct you in what you are to do and when you are to do it. —

—Why? —Castle said.

Vargas's eyes flared but he didn't lash out. There. There it was. Castle was right. That moment of hesitation, the slot where, for a second, he would negotiate. Vargas said,

—There is a revolution coming, a very violent and bloody revolution. You will be an instrument of that revolution. You. —

—Thank you, — Castle said.

Vargas's mouth opened in a smile, then vanished leaving only the cruel hard line of a man immersed in death. He said,

"You are a persistent son of a bitch. Or you are an idiot."

EIGHTEEN

Colonel Rodriguez entered behind two Nacionales lugging two cardboard boxes and a bottle of aguardiente. Rodriguez was married to the bottle. Sitting at the table he would talk, forcing Castle to drink with him until Rodriguez fell into a catatonic stupor.

Castle came alert as the room, this time, filled with tension, rage, the kind of lopsided blinding of thought that occurs when a madman is present. He shied away from Rodriguez, feeling danger the way you feel a needle in your eye. Not even the Nacionales had grown used to Rodriguez's drunkenness, his hard biting command.

They lit the kerosene lamp, set it on the table and waited.

Juanito, who had brought Castle to the room, averted his eyes. He had shrunk. He was not the same man he been earlier. Men, in Rodriguez's presence, changed. Losing more than their dignity.

Rodriguez took the bottle and waved the men out.

Closing the door with his boot, he staggered into the middle of the room, slammed the bottle against the table.

He stank of brandy. Head tilted forward, chin against his chest, he peered at Castle through thick eyebrows, his liquid black eyes flickering. Castle sensed that everything about Rodriguez had changed since his last visit.

— All right, — Rodriguez said. — The wait is over. —

He slavered. Drool poured from the sides of his mouth, white globs that he licked with his tongue.

He opened one of the boxes. Stern. Solemn faced and deliberate. Yes. He had changed. He coughed. Lit a cigarette.

— These are your toys. You pick.—

Castle inspected the box. He felt energy flowing from Rodriguez. Jets of power, overwhelming. He knew the feeling, had felt it many times in competition. It was the scent of challenge.

— How big are your balls, Castle? —Rodriguez mumbled.

He slid his pistol from its holster and stood waving it like a wand.

From the box, Castle pulled out four hand grenades, a machine pistol, and a machete in its leather sheath.

The kerosene lamp filled the room with a yellowish light that deepened shadows and worked on faces like a paintbrush turning skin into masks, teeth into fangs, hands into clawed instruments of fear.

Castle held the machine pistol as Rodriguez pointed his pistol at him.

— Pick? Why? — Castle said.

— How much man are you? —

Rodriguez muttered. He laughed. The laugh made him cough. He said,

— You're going on a holy mission. Can you do it? —

Castle set the grenades on the table. He laid the machine pistol down beside the grenades then rummaged inside the box. He said,

—Ammo? —

Rodriguez sneered. His mouth a black slit. His eyes were wild, he raised the pistol. Castle paid no attention but he felt the ache in the man's trigger finger. He didn't understand. He said,

— What do I do? —

—Yes. What do you do? You suck cock. —

Rodriguez laughed. He aimed the pistol at Castle, held it there. Then tottering he lifted one booted foot and propped it on a chair. The pistol hung across his leg, pointed now at the floor. Rodriguez squinted at his wristwatch.

—Later tonight. Later. Tonight, you will be allowed to perform a sacred act of devotion. —

— Devotion? —

— Some communists will be meeting in Huañuscacuchu. A meeting that's only going to happen once. —

— What am I going to do? —

— You never know who's a communist,— Rodriguez said. —You think your friends are true, but then you learn that they are communist pigs and they all have to be slaughtered. You will slaughter them and then you will return here. —

— And then what? —.

— You return here. —

Rodriguez reached into his tunic pocket, came up empty, shifted the pistol to the other hand, felt in another pocket and tossed a packet on the table. Castle picked it up, held it in the light. It contained his passport, a plane ticket to Rio and several thousand dollars in bills of a hundred.

— This will be waiting for you after you kill the communist atheists pricks. This is an impure world and not very often do you get a chance to purify it. I envy you.

We are not safe. When people who were your friends turn out to be communists, who can you trust? —

— So I slaughter them and return here. —

— Vargas says you will be allowed to leave when you have completed this task. I don't want to let you go because I think you're a fucking communist too. You should all be killed. Communists, Yankees, imperialists, predatory capitalists, Masons, all communist animals to be slaughtered to make the world safe for human beings. —

— I will need ammunition for this pistol if I am to slaughter these pigs. —

— You can kill them with the spirit of Jesus Christ our Lord and savior, — Rodriguez slurred his words. —He is so mighty and pure that communist swine tremble when the soldiers of God mention his name. Do you believe in God? Do you believe in the pure blood of Jesus Christ? Do you believe in the Saints? You're not a soldier of God...I can see it in your eyes. You are a pagan Indian... To me, Castle, you're just another Indian. You can dress how you want, you can act how you want, you can speak all those languages but with that skin and that nose you're just another Indian and you'll die like every other Indian. —

— Ammunition? —

—If you were a real man you wouldn't use this kind of weapon. You'd use the machete. But you're not a soldier of God. I don't trust you, Castle. Vargas says you will do this, but I think you don't have the balls to do it. I think you're a communist pig faggot, that's what I think. —

Castle peered at the Colonel. He picked up one of the hand grenades. He said,

— You don't trust me, why do you set me free to do this? —

— I don't trust you. And I'm not setting you free. You'll be watched. Vargas wills it. —

— Where will I do what he asks? —

— I'll take you there. —

—You want me to kill these men...—

— They aren't men. —

Rodriguez looked puzzled, his face skewed to one side, his watery black eyes seemed to focus then go blank.

—They are communists. I can smell communists. They have the odor of sick animals. —

Castle took a deep breath. He said,

— Why don't you have your dogs do it for you? You don't need me. —

— Because everyone would know, — Rodriguez said. —We know everything that happens in Ayahuantu, therefore people assume we do everything that ever gets done. There have been many governments in the Americas and all of them have been betrayed by the communists to the Yankees. Yankees think they own what is ours. They don't believe in God. They are communist too. Everyone must die. You, I, my men must if it will rid the world of these communist anti-christ insect swine. —

Rodriguez smiled. Drank from the bottle. Coughed.

— Ah but you, Castle. You look like another Indian piece of shit, but Vargas says that you will kill them, and if you do that then I have only to arrest you and justice is done. Everyone knows what happens when you disappear in Ayahuantu. —

Rodriguez laughed. He said,

— You know, don't you? We liquify the disappeared. Turn them back into water. That Indian body you live in is just water and some chemicals. But did you know that communist insect swine don't feel pain the way human beings do? They can't feel pain because they don't believe in the cleansing blood of Jesus Christ who died for our sins. —

— Why these men? —

—They are not men. They are communists. They challenge Vargas. They challenge Vargas who has been sent by God to wipe clean this community of anti-christ pig-urine. Vargas has been chosen by God to rid our land of the swine, and they are against Vargas, just as the Yankees are against Vargas so they too are Reds who must die. —

—Who are these communist swine and where are they that I can kill them? —

— Swine. You learn quickly. Maybe you aren't a communist. Maybe you're just a faggot. They are all where all worms are. They're intestinal parasites rotting our insides, eating us up from within. Fungus eating our brain. If only the world were not such a complex affair. Unfortunately, God in his infinite wisdom created it complex to perplex us, or it has grown into complexity and we have gotten stupid and so it vexes us? Vargas is not stupid. In any case no man can understand how it works and if he did he would go mad when he asked why it should be so. There are things we know , and some that we should not. —

Rodriguez coughed hard. He looked at Castle. He said,

— Vargas says you will kill these swine who have no names. Only human beings have names. Does a pig have a name? Does a worm have a name? Does shit have a name?—

— You want me to kill them, but I do not know their names. —

— When I first saw you with Everett, I knew you were a faggot. A cowardly faggot but Everett was a friend to Vargas, he was not a communist , and you were with Everett, so you might not be a communist but you can still be a faggot and that means you could also be a communist and maybe that is why Everett died. He was a Yankee and the Yankees are communist, and they will betray us the way our other friends have now betrayed us. An event is about to take place, Castle. It is not a revolution because that word ought to be reserved for the moment of liberation when the human spirit becomes one with Jesus Christ , the great moment when the will of God is imposed on earth. That is our duty, but first all communists must be destroyed to purify the earth to prepare us for the Kingdom of God. And if we all have to die, then we have to die. —

Castle reached for the table, fingered the machete that was still in its sheath. He said,

— Dreams of empire, Colonel? Vargas has dreams of empire? —

— This is a poor country surrounded by communist giants. We have had to creep through time with our necks bowed. But in the earth there is promise for the first time that a generation of my people can be born who will not live in this poverty. Vargas has promised that we will not be laughed at by our neighbors and pointed at by communist tourists who laugh at our quaint and curious and backward ways. No. Not dreams of empire. Vargas dreams of equality. And to achieve it, your sacrifice is small in comparison. —

— These men, these communists, these swine I will kill threaten God's vision for Vargas? —

— Unfortunately, yes. The promise is not for today. It is the future and must be protected for people so that when they emerge from their long night of sorrow and suffering, there will be a time for them. The wealth of the earth will be forged into a weapon that will not betray us. Friends betray us. They become communist, but we will not be tainted with greed. We must control our wealth and guard it from the Reds, no matter what disguise they give themselves. They are communist and some of them disguise themselves as Ayahuantuan. But we know who they are. With Jesus leading us, our tiny and insignificant country will emerge into the next millennium with a special sword forged by the hand of god and we will become once more protectors of the faith. —

—And Vargas is the man who will build this weapon and deliver your country from the communists? —

—The man who guides the people must come from the earth which comes from God and he must take his power from the earth which is God's gift to man. Whoever controls the soil controls the future of Ayahuantu and when we have the weapon all of America will fear us. Tiny though we are, we will be heard and our voice will be thunder. It is unfortunate, but not all the landowners agree with Vargas in who should exercise control, but of course they have all become communist. Still the weapon will one day be ours. Everett was working with us to secure that finality, but now it has become impossible to proceed in the manner Vargas had planned, so action must be taken. It is very complex. Many people now know what lies in the earth at Llapa Atipac, but they do not have the interest of Ayahuantu at heart and so they must die. All of them. They have only their own greed and selfish interests at heart, Castle, communist interest, Yankee interests, capitalist interest and the landlords are no longer willing to follow Vargas but have brought corruption into our country. They offer gifts but exact such a price that we cannot accept. —

— And Chacanahuayco? — Castle said. –Everett knew what is there?

—Of course Everett knew about Chananahuayco. —

—He didn't tell me what Vargas is building there. —

—Vargas is building the future there and from there we will direct the strikes, but that is not of interest to you. —

—Is Centrex going to build the reactor? Are Centrex leaders among the Faithful? —

—Yes, Everett was one of the Faithful. But we were betrayed. We did not know that the short man...—

—Jacobs? Cathay? —

—Jacobs betrayed Vargas to Cathay and the communists know everything. —

Castle ran his thumb over the machete's edge. Rodriguez coughed. His black alcoholic eyes runny, his mustache flecked with spittle. The pistol hung limp in his hand, aimed to the floor. He said,

—You must go. It is time. —

—Where are we going? —

—To a house in Huañuscacuchu. —

—The communist swine are there? —

—Yes, in the house of the dwarf. —

The dwarf? The dwarf was Villareal. Villareal who owned Llapa Atipac. Castle wanted more. He watched Rodriguez, saw malignancy in the Colonel's eyes, in the face waves of cruelty rippled out in circles the way an open can of poison soils the air. Rodriguez said,

—Before we go, Vargas told me to give you this. —

Rodriguez kicked the second cardboard box, sending it skittering across the floor. The kerosene lamp flickered, flaring bright, then dimming to a pale yellow. Rodriguez's heavy face appeared bloated. He said,

—We found it yesterday. A gift from your communist friends. —

Castle inserted the machete under the twine binding the lid of the box. He pushed the lid off.

There, staring up at him, hollow eyed and gray, his penis protruding from its mouth, lay the severed head of Onorato.

*****

In the jeep, Rodriguez gave Castle names. Names that he recited as a death-litany and Castle absorbed them. As they drove, Castle smelled the scent of the night the way an insect searches for a mate. As the list ended, Castle knew he would start with Marta. She had betrayed him to Jacobs and she might call him again, but this time she would die before the name came out of her mouth. Jacobs would die. Marta would die. Cathay would die. It was the smell of death that drove Castle now.

Rodriguez dropped Castle halfway down Villareal's street. In his left hand, Castle carried the head of Onorato and in his right, the machete still in its sheath. Rodriguez said,

—Return to Hidalgo when you finish. No one will meet you. —

A dozen automobiles lined Villareal's street. Large German and French machines. Diseased American vehicles built for men and women whose feet never touched Ayanuantuan earth. Lumbering vehicles that came out at night with their occupants crouched behind blackened glass hiding from the eyes of the Indians. Exotic and stupid animals, they nested against the curb waiting to be slaughtered.

There were drivers in uniforms, parasites who sucked the blood of the rich as the rich sucked the blood of the Indians.

And there was one jeep drawn up on the sidewalk by the gate.

Vic.

*****

Castle waits in the shadows, no more than a shadow, Onorato's head dangling from his left hand, the machete at his side. He is aflame with the power bursting inside him as he is called to do something unearthly—to rid Ayahuantu of its parasites.

*****

The machete is two feet of fingernail forged into a steel blade that fits the hand—mayhem disguised as a tool.

*****

Castle searches for the white helmets, the black jeeps, but the insects are not there.

He is become silence. He has no words. No thoughts.

Language has left him, forcing him to forage through the primitive movements of some entity deeper buried in him than his humanity.

Slithering through the night, the head of Onorato hanging from his hand, Castle, comes to a halt on a side street.

*****

Drawn from its holster, a pistol leaves no doubt of its meaning. Unlike the pistol, the machete is an ambiguous device. That is its strength, its appeal, its horror.

*****

Waiting is not now in his flesh. To wait is to die. He, the instrument, will rust if he rests. He lifts the head, peers into the vacant eyes, a sensation blooms in his head—a picture of a man, like every man— rising and the eyes blink, saying yes.

Grunting, he glides through the street in a wide arc, sliding through shadows, guided to the door Onorato had opened for him in his escape. *When did they butcher you, my friend?*

*****

In its sheath, the machete is no threat, for it is then seen as a tool. Unsheathed, it still is not yet a deadly weapon. That is its beauty and its terror.

*****

The stable door. A blank wall of fitted planks. Castle draws the machete and splits the planks. The wood groans in its old age, nails squeal from their blooded graves.

*****

In a hand, the blade is a claw-like and gruesome weapon, not a polished gleaming machine, but a simple strip of hammered steel fitted into a clumsy handle wrapped with rough-cut leather. Not a tool for cutting, but an eruption from the hinges of time.

*****

Through the stable rich with its earthy, musty scents of labor and sweat, Castle moves into the garden. A garden reeking thick with exotic night flowers. Machete in hand Castle approaches the house, hears voices. He stops, looks into the kitchen. Open windows. Indian women working, talking, hands moving, trays of food, bottles of drink.

*****

The machete can cut a field of sugarcane or blaze a trail through thickets. It is a comfort, an ally facing the elements. When the canes are arms and necks and the crop is flesh, the machete becomes a walking plague that sends dread through men.

*****

A door opens. Cathay in a group of short men with fair skin and balding heads, landowners who fit in the limousines with their thin fair-skinned, high-heeled women, women who speak no mother tongue but are fluent in the language of greed. The door closes. Cathay. Random flickers of Cathay in a hotel room giving Castle to Jacobs who gave him to the men who kissed only one love and her name is pain.

*****

Honed, the machete is a hymn to devastation. Sharpened, it is death singing on a pendulum, entering and leaving the flesh like music through the mind, propelled by its own weight, while bone is a minor obstacle as the heft of the steel, transformed into hurt, arcs through and out even before blood can leap up, brilliant, from the wound.

*****

Landowners. Born into it. Castle grasps Onorato's head, turns it over. The butchering has altered it. Toothless now. Lacerated flesh. Wounds clotted with grime. Castle soothes away the detritus, holds the head as a deep relic. The eyes are dull. The work of landowners. The lips are blackened. The gift of landowners. Castle strokes the machete, not taking his eyes from Onorato's empty eyes.

****

The machete in the hand of a man who knows its history, puts the fear of the angel of death into even the bravest warrior.

*****

On his feet, moving through the serving women watching him come out of the night blood-covered and near-naked, the Indian head held by the hair, and in his hand the machete. Seeing him, they do not scream or shout as though they recognize him as an avatar of revenge not come for them but to restore balance in the world.

*****

At close quarters, the machete is magic. Better than any firearm. More dependable than a dagger. More brutal than a bayonet.

*****

Women, in silence, return, eyes down, to their work and Castle bursts through the door-of-the-servants into the heart of greed, the machete living at the end of his arm cuts first shining through silk then through flesh and brightened emerges coated with the first corruption of patrician bone. A living shadow moving, Castle becomes willful steel. Women in silk and satin screaming cannot mask the song of the blade as it melts into long-awaited home.

*****

Cutting edge up, the machete is a god-hammer. It crushes without cutting, maims without spilling blood, cripples without opening flesh. It smashes, it cuts. It never breaks.

*****

There are eight men with their women in the elegant room, patricians of rich size and shape and color, but they all fall dumb as destruction spins through their ranks, reducing richness and greed to body parts skimming across the wooden and ancient floors. Castle is a snarling beast—three dead then four then five and Castle stands before Cathay whose eyes widen as Castle raises the blade, arcing it, a flat whirling circle of steel that silences the scream before it can clear the larynx denying Cathay his final insult.

*****

Stupid men believing legends of their own bravery as long as their fingers rest on steel triggers, stupid men whimper when an intense and angry Indian rises out of the darkness flashing a machete. And that is the last thing they ever see. The whimper stops in the throat, the neck bursts, head severed by this hand-held guillotine.

*****

Cathay stands, not yet realizing that this toothless, bloody, horrid wraith has murdered him. In two pieces—one tumbling in disarray to the floor, the other erect, atwitch, spurting life in pulsing geysers then, flailing, writhes its final act.

*****

In an unjust world, the machete is the court of justice for those who have no recourse to judges. When a man takes it up as a weapon, he announces that the justice of civilized society is moribund. For those seeking redress for crimes against them, the machete metes out retribution and, like all that is good, it is swift.

*****

Some try to flee through locked doors—women seeking repentance—but peasant justice finds them, six seven now eight. The quickness of the blade leaves no time for deliberation and then, there is Jacobs in a doorway, pistol in hand. He crouches, aims the weapon, but before he can squeeze, the flying head of Onorato takes him down and Castle rakes the claw of metal across Jacobs' throat and Jacobs' eyes darken and Jacobs' blood darkens the air as his head lies against Onorato's abused and destroyed head.

*****

The machete does not dignify death. There can be no honor in falling to a tool. The machete allows no moral victory in defeat but heaps humiliation on victims while gaining silent revenge for the assailant.

*****

Castle discovers Villareal behind a chair, whimpering, eyes fixed on the blade. Centuries before, death had been in those eyes but now he yields saying, by his surrender, that he will die at that hand of his sins. He rises, lays upon the steel, as if remembering the sword of his ancestors buried in the flesh of a conquered people. There is little blood in the body of a decaying patrician.

Marta kneels on the floor beside a dead woman in silk and pearls.

Castle pounces on her, grasps the white hair, yanks at the neck of the black dress baring the throat and he raises the machete. But there is no fear in her eyes.

—Not me, — she says. —I am not one of them. —

Castle recognizes in her, beyond the sound coming from the mouth, something so cruel, so deep, so full of animal power that he hesitates.

—Kill them all, — Rodriguez had said.

—I am the Faithful, — Marta says.

She kneels. Looks up at him with the eyes of a supplicant imploring her god to save her.

Raising the machete, Castle turns the blade into a hammer and smashes it into her and she collapses to the floor, mouth open. She says,

—I am the Faithful. —

The second blow cuts the life from her and her white head rolls.

Castle picks up Onorato, the butchered purity, and he glances around at his work and he sees the silk and pearls, the diamonds in blood, the thighs now spread revealing useless nakedness. He sees the shine of costly shoes smattered with redness and he sees the tailored luxury of wool cloth tortured by the blade. He sees the bodies of strange animals—fanged, bloated beasts reeking with gore. He sees skin cut open and from the wounds crawl venomous insects and unspeakable species of vermin. White things on the floor ooze—not blood but pus and slime, the residue of rapacious alien creatures—bloating and cracking open and there, the one with white hair, now headless, gutted like a very large queen of an ancient and decaying world spews eggs from her belly.

BLOOD

Holding Onorato close, Castle turned to the door as a rippling of thunder tore open the silence. A bite into his flesh.

The door opened and Vic, a cadre of four khaki-shirted snakes behind him, slid into the death-hall waving a machine-pistol and Castle, seeing the surprise in the old man's eyes, swung the machete and it arced out and Vic was dead and then Castle waded through the armed men who froze as if the waves of death had slammed into them before the machete itself seethed through their bones.

Castle felt exultation run through him and as he entered the night, the night pressed its gentle darkness over him and he knew that the blackening blood caking him was drying and cracking and falling away from him—sloughing itself away, skin of a viper molting.

Hidalgo. Waiting in Hidalgo was his blood money. He said to Onorato,

—We have bought our return with their blood, my friend. —

The Turks murder a million and a half Armenians, and nobody says
I'm sorry. The Nazis murder six million Jews and nobody says I'm
sorry. The Americans slaughter a three hundred thousand Japanese with
one bomb but nobody beats his chest and cries "My fault!" The Khmer
Rouge massacre a million Cambodians and nobody cries out loud. Mao
murders twenty-five million Chinese, but who apologizes for him?
Stalin puts away another twenty million Russians without a blush. What
the hell! I kill one lousy Ayahuantuan poet, who wasn't even very
good and you want me to fall on my knees and do a thousand mea culpas?
This is no century for apologies. Who's going to listen to you if you
say I'm sorry anyway? Who? No one. This is no century for apologies.

About Jack Remick

Jack Remick is a novelist and a poet. His work has appeared around the country.

Coffeetown Press published *The California Quartet—The Deification, Valley Boy, The Book of Changes,* and *Trio of Lost Souls.*

Gabriela and The Widow was a finalist for the Montaigne Award.

Blood, a companion novel to *No Century for Apologies* and *Doubles in a Game of Chance,* was published by Camel Press, an imprint of Coffeetown.

Remick is co-author, with Robert J. Ray, of *The Weekend Novelist Writes a Mystery.*

Remick's poetry includes *Josie Delgado, a poem of the Central Valley, Satori—Poems,* and work in *The Seattle Five Plus One.*

He has other work in various anthologies including *Raven Chronicles V/ 26, The Helicon West Anthology,* and *So Much Depends Upon,* (a Red Wheelbarrow Writers Anthology).